It Happened

at The Green Room

~*~

Marissa Benning

Jill Bodach

N. Apythia Morges

A.J. O'Connell

Tamela J. Ritter

Erika K. Zamek

This is a work of fiction. Names, characters, places and incidents are either the product of the author's imagination or are used fictitiously, and any resemblance to actual persons, living or dead, business establishments, events, or locales is entirely coincidental.

IT HAPPENED AT THE GREEN ROOM

Printing history:
2007 BookSurge The Green Room Edition

ISBN: 1-4196-6713-0
ISBN 13: 978-1-41966713-8

Printed in the United States of America

We dedicate this book to Mr. Schmitty who brightened the evenings and warmed the laps of the regulars since Kathy brought him in from the streets of Bridgeport and adopted him as the best bar cat around.

The bar will never be the same without you!

Table of Contents

The Stories

The Introduction

Tamela: One night while sorting through how exactly my life had fallen to shit, I received a call from a friend, whose life was also falling to shit. "Hey, ya wanna get a drink and bitch about how our lives are shit?"

"Why yes, I do like to talk about my life turning to shit, and I do enjoy drinking. Sounds perfect, where in Fairfield County can we find a place to do both these things?"

"The Green Room, meet me in an hour."

That began our sojourn at the Green Room. We recruited our other friends who decided that instead of talking about our lives falling to shit, we actually do something to change it.

So one night while sitting in the back room, staring at the likeness of Tom Waits and relying on board game for writing inspiration, we decided to seek inspiration from the patrons themselves.

~*~

A.J.: One night, my life fell to shit. Seeing this, I decided to leave my apartment. But before I did, I called a friend and told her to meet me at the only place I knew I would be truly fine; a bar I used to spend time at before my life began its transition to shit. The Green Room, as I remembered it, was an antique store of a bar, where everything from the furniture to the art on the walls was for sale; a place where I once met a friend I knew during my days as a student in Spain. Thus began the second chapter of my hanging at the Green Room.

Other friends joined us in the next week, and when we tired of playing cards, we played pool, and when we tired playing pool we wrote stories, and when we tired of that, we decided to write a book about the regulars we met there every Wednesday and this book was born.

~*~

Erika: One afternoon when I was feeling overwhelmed by the descent of my life toward the rather unappealing status of shit, I opened my inbox to find a message from one of my girls with a callout to head up to the Green Room, even though it was an "off" week. And I thought: *I think that I will go up, too. I could use a drink and some company.* It was the beginning of the end—the end of my sanity, the end of my self-imposed solitude, and the end—well, *almost* the end—of my fears about whether or not I belonged with this "Unholy Handful." It wasn't my first visit to the Green Room, my fifth, or even my tenth. But it was the night that I found my writing family, and I wouldn't trade them for all the tea in China. That is seriously saying something, since I absolutely adore tea.

So when my family came up with this awesome idea to create a collection of stories inspired by the intriguing people that lived in this wonderfully chaotic place that we'd made our home, I embraced the scheme wholeheartedly and with zeal. After all…who could not get head-over-heels excited about an idea like this?

~*~

Jill: I'm proud to say that while my life has often hung precariously over large puddles of shit, it's never actually been immersed in the stuff – but that doesn't mean I haven't been provided with my share of fodder for stories that seek to amuse, disturb, entice and entertain. I've been writing these stories in the form of novels, short stories and poems since I was seven. My mother has always told me that I am a brilliant writer. This still remains the highest praise I've ever received in my writing career, but I'm hopeful that there will be more, preferably from someone other than the woman who bore me (no offense Mom).

Anyway, it was that desire for feedback on my work that led me to join these lovely ladies at the Green Room. We'd all previously been in a writing group together but after two years we sought the comfort of a smaller group - and a place where we could drink while we wrote. Writers on the Rocks was born. Each week we came to the Green Room, fell into the chairs and onto the couches and shared inspiration for stories – and more than a few laughs.

This project came to life Labor Day weekend 2006 in a small cabin in Pennsylvania – and I do mean small. We spent our days writing and asking ourselves questions like, "If you were to have sex on a pool table…" We spent our nights drinking and singing obnoxiously loud Billy Joel's "Only the Good Die Young." And this book you hold in your hands is what we created.

~*~

Apythia: As I was going through a divorce, it goes without saying that my life was shit. So when Tam and A.J. invited me to come to the Green Room on Thanksgiving 2005 to play trivia and drink, I was so there. And so began the Green Room post-holiday drinking binge, which evolved into the Wednesday drinking binge which eventually became the hey-we-should-probably-do-some-writing-while-we-drink binge. And thus, Writers on the Rocks was born.

Now it should be pointed out that our little group likes to come up with schemes, uhm, I mean ideas, to expand our writing. And like all great ideas, this one was conceived in the bathroom of the Green Room . While staring at the posters littering the wall, I had an epiphany and rushed out to the girls – thankfully not trailing toilet paper – and within the hour, we had outlined the project for this book and put things in motion that would make us laugh, cry, bitch, moan and even bleed. But we did it for the love of writing. And drinking.

The Writers

~*~

MARISSA BENNING, from everywhere and nowhere, is a saucy vixen that spends her days writing and her nights beating bad boys into submission while downing bourbon or whiskey with an "E" straight from the bottle. Because of the explicit naughtiness of most of her work, her true identity is highly secret, just like that of her drinking partner A. Nonymous.

~*~

JILL BODACH's natural hair color is a secret closely guarded by the National Guard, the CIA, FBI, Secret Service, and KGB. She spends her days writing fluffy feature stories, studying and teaching literature, and waiting for Oprah to make her novel the next book-of-the-month pick. She doesn't like disco bowling and will not under any circumstances eat avocados or pickles. Her ideal drinking partner would be J.D. Salinger – if she could find him.

~*~

N. APYTHIA MORGES, of New York (formerly of Pennsylvania, England and North Carolina), dreams of owning a cottage in the English countryside where she can write at the local pub while enjoying a diet coke spiked with vanilla vodka and fantasizing about hot vampires, lycanthropes and snarky Potions masters while her muse gets pissed on cider with the locals. Any story she was in would have to involve some sort of fantasy/occult element in which she got to kick ass and make out with the sexier -than-sin leading man.

~*~

A.J. O'CONNELL, of Bridgeport, Connecticut, is the self-proclaimed hottest female nerd in the world. When she's not draining gin and tonics at her neighborhood bar, or blogging about how much Final Fantasy sucks, she is penning school bulletins and dreaming of quitting the life. If she had her druthers, A.J. would be written into a painfully clever story by Isaac Asimov as a charismatic anti-hero who turns out to be a robot.

~*~

TAMELA J. RITTER, of Spokane, Washington; Missoula, Montana; Houston, Texas; and Norwalk, Connecticut, likes to drink White Russians (if there's milk) and Tequila Sunrises (If the orange juice isn't a funky brown color) while talking about writing with "The Unholy Handful" at The Green Room. If she could be in any story she would be traveling the country with John Steinbeck and the story would be told by Tom Robbins and would be called "Travels with Johnny."

~*~

ERIKA K. ZAMEK is an environmental geochemist by day and budding fantasy/romance/adventure writer by night. Her indecisive tendencies are exacerbated by the Baileys Irish Cream that she prefers to share with her literary crush of the moment. If she could step into the pages of a story, Erika would be the tough yet vulnerable heroine in a Melanie Rawn-esq tapestry who uses her wits and fantastical magic to destroy her arch-nemesis.

The Players

ARIANNA (a.k.a. The Beaver), 30, of Stratford, slings back Velvet Vaginas after working as a jailhouse nurse. In her story, she would be carrying on a secret love affair with the proprietor of the Green Room and they would finally succumb to their desires on the pool table.

~*~

THE BANKER, 35, of Bridgeport, would discuss debaucheries with the Marquis de Sade over Seven and Seven. His story would be a black comedy in which he'd be the syphilitic whore with a heart of gold who looked like Abe Vigoda in 1953 Algiers, and in which a cucumber disappeared.

~*~

CARLOS, (aka Los, Losballs, Balls) 25, of Trumbull, would like to enjoy Red Stripe, Bass and whiskey with a horny, drunk female version of himself. When he isn't at the bar, he likes to play music, work, and destroy France. In his dark comedy or war drama, he would be an evil chair builder with funny stories in either the Roaring Twenties of present-day Portugal.

~*~

CHACHI, 27, of Devon, would love to have an Effen & Tonic with Graham Chapman. His story would be an epic adventure in which he would be the wacky, loveable sidekick, a scallywag with braided chest hairs. The story would take place 420 years in the future, when Zack Morris would rise from the grave and become supreme ruler of the universe. The hero and Chachi would defeat him.

~*~

THE COMRADE, 29, of Westport, dreams of drinking pretty much anything with George Bush, Sr. and Dr. Dre while he spins a yarn about his days as a character in a detective noir story where he "roots out enemies of world workers' unity amongst the rich and powerful."

~*~

COWBOY, 42, of Bridgeport, would raise a beer to Herodotus and Arilla when he wasn't working, reading, sleeping or riding. In his 1984 continental U.S.A. comedy, he would be a mentor, an older Odysseus who takes a younger, very cynical Telemachus on the Great American Road Trip and teaches him to love our country.

DREW, 28, of Newtown, would like to drink Maker's Mark Bourbon on the rocks with Johnny Depp and Mitch Hedberg. He wants to be an obnoxious drunk with "Fabio-like hair" in his violent comedy.

~*~

THE GOVERNOR, (not THE Gov.), of Bridgeport, dreams of swilling a rum and coke with Captain Hook when he isn't recovering from hangovers. His story would be a tragedy involving a dress in which he played the town drunk and Teedius or Quizno's would be the setting in this story that brings doom to all.

~*~

THOMAS JAMES KANE was too drunk to tell us much about himself. Based on his behavior that night, we surmised that he had never been at the Green Room before and usually spends his time lying on the side of the road. In the story of his life, he plays the Gimp and look a bit like Ron Jeremy as he satisfies his friends' wives.

~*~

JUNIOR, (Big Boy), 32, of Bridgeport, has been hanging out at the bar for five years and is still waiting to share a rum and coke with the Pope. He wants to be a terminator-like assassin in the future in his story.

~*~

MICHAEL, (aka Pocketbook Boy, Johnny Dakota, George P and Neil Greco), 28, of Bridgeport, would treat Ben Franklin to a beer or whiskey. His tall tale would feature Ben, in which he'd make a cameo. The story would start fun and ended horribly in December of 1943.

~*~

THE PROPRIETOR, (Sister Sandra), 40, of Bridgeport, when she is not running the bar, is running screaming into the ocean, awaiting her drinking partner Bilbo Baggins, and drinking Absolut Citron. She would like a story were she is an ass-kicking warrior princess in medieval times.

The Stories

JUNIOR AND THE GEEK

~*~

A.J. O'Connell

Author's Notes: The inspiration from this story came from, obviously, Junior and the Geek. (Chachi is the geek.) I wanted to give them both exactly what they asked for, including, but not limited to, braided chest hairs.

~*~

The year is 2426, and in a laboratory, on an island, which 200 years ago was the top of a mountain, thousands of young men in white coats are slaving away over huge metal tubs filled with viscous materials while a gigantic portrait of their god hangs on the wall above, his sacred winning smile illuminating the room. The workers are white, they are fresh-faced, they are blonde and seem to be trying to imitate a mischievous, yet endearing overconfidence.

But the imitation is not enough, and that is why they work night and day at their tasks, striving towards a dream that has taken decades to achieve. They are so close, now. So close.

In one of the vats, something begins to bubble, then starts to boil.

"It's beginning," screams one scientist, "The time has finally come!!"

The lab falls silent. There is no noise except the bubbling in the vat. One hundred pairs of Aryan blue eyes turn upwards, in prayer, to the picture hanging on the wall.

"We must tell the Principal," murmurs someone.

Cuarto Verde was the sort of bar that could sit on a main thoroughfare and not be noticed for years by a native. It was the kind of place you might find yourself in at night somehow, but you never noticed it during the day unless you woke up there at 11 a.m. after being on a weeklong bender.

Which is how Chachi usually saw it. That's why, at 10:30 on a rainy workday, Junior Perrogrande was standing on Fourth Main Street on the Fourth Tier of New Bridgeport (it was a tall city), peering in through the dark plate glass windows of Cuarto Verde. Sure enough, there was Chachi, passed out on the floor in front of the bar.

Junior cursed, and stormed up a nearby flight of asphalt stairs to Fifth Main Street. The city's Fifth Tier was a little more residential than the Fourth, lined with plain concrete buildings with metal doors. Junior whaled on one of them with his fist for a full minute before an intercom clicked on.

"Diga," said a woman's sleepy voice. She sounded as if she were taking a pull off a cigarette.

"Maria, open up, damn it."

Junior waited, seething, until the door slid into the wall, revealing a thin blonde woman wearing a pink bathrobe and a very irritated expression.

"Did you have to leave him on the floor, Maria? Could you at least have put him on a couch?"

The thin woman snorted smoke out her nose and rifled through her keys before stepping outside and heading down the stairs.

"I'll tell you what," she said. "Next time, I'll just prop him up outside so you don't have to come wake me up. How's that?"

Junior didn't respond, just waited for Maria to raise the door. From where he was standing he could see that his friend was breathing – in fact he could smell that his friend breathing.

I don't want to have to do this again, Junior," Maria said from the door of the bar, as he carried Chachi down the stairs towards the Second Tier. "You hear me?"

"Piss off," Junior muttered under his breath.

The crowds thickened as he descended to the Third Tier and then again to the Second. New Bridgeport wasn't a huge city, but it was a significant port, built right over the steadily rising ocean (Main Street on the First Tier was already a foot underwater) and connected to the mainland by a very long bridge. As a result, the city was often full of travelers, traders and sailors.

A blond fresh-faced young sailor bumped against Junior as the big man descended into the Second Tier. Junior scowled as they made eye contact.

"Sorry, Mack," the sailor said, smiling cheekily, until the unconscious Chachi caught his eye. He stared for a second.

"Piss off," muttered Junior, starting to haul Chachi back down the flight of stairs.

"Cool!" responded the sailor brightly, and made his way up the stairs, turning every few steps to stare back at Chachi.

"Freaky bastard," muttered Junior and hefted Chachi onto Second Main Street and down a side street, Pausing to unlock a door before dragging his burden into a small apartment, down a hall, through a bathroom and into a tub already filled with ice-cold water.

Chachi gulped air and thrashed, rising half out of the tub. Junior pushed him back in with one foot. Eventually Chachi seemed to recognize his surroundings, because he stopped kicking and began shivering and shaking his head a little.

"Junior, I think I'm still drunk," he said in amazement, looking at the bathroom wide-eyed and making another attempt to get out of the tub.

Junior shoved him back down.

"How long was I out?" asked Chachi, continuing his struggle to leave the bathtub.

Junior pushed him down.

"Where did you find me?"

Another shove back down.

"I can't remember anything."

Shoved down again.

"This is really cold."

He splashed back down into the bathtub again, and eyed Junior's boot, which was on his shoulder.

"Junior, I don't feel so good."

Junior removed his boot and turned on his heel.

"You don't smell so good either," he said. "There's water and aspirin on the counter. Don't bang on the door until you're clean *and* sober. And make sure the bathroom is clean, too."

He left, locking the door behind him and walked into the main room of his apartment, which looked more like an armory than a living room. Guns and ammo hung from the walls, a weight machine squatted in the corner where you might expect to find a bed. Junior stalked to the fridge, pulled out the milk and swigged from the carton. There were grenades in the crisper.

He was not in a good mood, but that wasn't unusual. Junior was only in a good mood when he was working, and New Bridgeport didn't have much to offer a professional assassin in the way of work. Oh sure, there were the occasional political refugees coming into port, stowaway criminals and other illegal passengers, that sort of thing. But they were few and far between, and they were just survival kills. It was so bad that Junior had to schedule one or two "big game hunts" as he liked to call them – expeditions on the mainland, netting big kills, which provided enough money for him to live on the rest of the year. His walls were covered in trophies from these hunts; a lock of hair, a torn shirt, a leather glove.

It would be time for one of these expeditions soon, he thought. And for that, he would need his little buddy, sobering up in the bathroom. Chachi might be tall, scrawny and funny looking, but he was one hell of a diversion when Junior was on the job. Which is the only reason why Junior went looking for him in the first place. He needed Chachi to be able to work.

Junior heard a screech from the bathroom. He turned away but then figured he may as well check it out. Opening the door he discovered his friend, head in his hands, leaning on the sink, his shirt hanging open.

"I must have been really drunk," he groaned when the door swished open, and turned toward Junior, exposing his chest. The hair was braided in neat circular cornrows around his nipples.

"Just clean up," said Junior, and locked him in the bathroom again. "I'm going out."

He walked out into the street and headed back to Second Main Street. It was busier than usual today – a couple large freighters had come into port, and the sailors, glad to be off their ships, were running up and down the streets and stairs, most of them heading up to the Third Tier, where the bridge to the mainland was. New Bridgeport was land, but not really. Lots of the guys actually liked to feel dirt under their boots. As he headed through the streets of the Second Tier towards The New Bridgeport Diner, Junior saw more blond sailors running roguishly through the streets.

Must be a ship in from Germany, thought Junior, pushing through a crowd of tow-headed troublemakers almost half his height, rounding a corner and ducking into a small metal building lined with windows. He was hungry. He had wasted his breakfast hour finding Chachi, and the lack of food was making him even crankier than he was regularly. At six foot six, Junior was a lot bigger than most people in the world and it took a lot of processed meat to fill him up.

The New Bridgeport Diner was the kind of place where you get exactly that much meat for less money than it cost to buy a cup of coffee in most restaurants. The wait staff saw Junior coming through the window and signaled the cook to start breakfast. It was that kind of place.

Junior spent most of his long brunch in silence, mulling over his upcoming expedition to the mainland. Usually he at least had an idea of whom he was going after, but this time no one had contacted him about a target, and there had been no advertisements for an assassin in The New Bridgeport Post for a long time. But Junior couldn't afford to wait much longer for an ad or a tip – the money was getting sparse and if he didn't find a target soon, he was going to have to start working security down at the docks.

His best bet, he decided, was to go hunting blind; to hit someone prominent and hope, after the fact, that person had enemies willing to pay for his or her demise.

Junior didn't like having to haggle for his price after the kill, but times were tough. He probably could have eliminated that problem by capturing his targets first, but he was dismal at kidnapping - it was easier to move a body when it wasn't trying to escape, and standing guard over a prisoner was tedious, and besides, begging and pleading always got to him. So he took his chances with killing a mark and haggling later, lying to make it sound as if the person were still alive and about to be killed that night, or relied on his appearance to encourage honesty in his clients.

All that remained, then, was to find his quarry. That would require research; something else that Junior was terrible at since he couldn't read.

Oh well, he thought, taking another bite of his large breakfast. That's another thing Chachi was good for.

Junior's reverie was broken when a small group of blond sailors came into the diner, laughing and fooling around good naturedly. Their devil-may-care attitude bothered him and he frowned down at his plate. To his chagrin, the waitress sat them near him. In a couple of minutes another young man in civilian clothes joined them. He was also blond, Junior noticed.

"Howya doin' Mack?" said one of the sailors to the new arrival.

The sailor didn't sound German, thought Junior.

The new guy high-fived everyone at the sailor's table, snapped his fingers and pointed at the waitress to beckon her over, and after they had all ordered their breakfasts in the most charming way imaginable, they abruptly dropped the act.

"Is it true?' asked the civilian blond, "Has he returned?"

"Yes," said one of the young men, his voice all of a sudden sounding kind of different from the others. "I have seen it. We have finally done it."

"Where is he?" the civilian sounded as if he might cry. "I must look upon him."

"Bay Side Lab," replied another sailor. "Patience. He is not ready yet. But we have been dispatched by The Principal to spread the word."

At the word principal all six bowed their heads and intoned: "You have a pal in the Principal."

Then another sailor continued: "When he is ready, he will command an army of thousands. We will be able to bring Coolness back to the planet."

The sailors paused reverentially but the civilian pressed on.

"And the others? His queen? What about them?"

"Not yet – we have not been able to bring back the other five," said one of them. "Although we may not have to bring back one…"

Junior could not believe his ears. His prayers had been answered. A returned leader who commands an army of thousands, someone called The Principal, a queen? A possible five other targets? This was great. It was the first he'd ever heard of this person, so it was a good bet he was the only assassin who knew about this new leader and his Coolness movement, or whatever. He even knew where the guy was – or he would, as soon as Chachi could figure out where the Bay Side Labs were. With as many blond cult members as this guy has, there must be someone who wants him dead, thought Junior.

Excitedly, he stood up, leaving enough coin on the bar to pay for brunch and dove into the foot traffic on the street. As he waded through the crowd on Second Main Street, Junior's mind raced with possibilities. Who was this guy? Royalty? Celebrity? It kind of sounded like he was a cult leader, and if Junior could stow away on the ship that had dumped a few hundred platinum blonds into his city, he might be taken right to him. The big man loped towards his apartment. He hoped Chachi was sobered up by now. Even if he weren't, Junior would probably have to release him from the bathroom and feed him if he wanted Chachi to get right on finding Bay Side Labs. Chachi might be annoying but he sure as hell was useful.

Junior came up short when he approached his place. The door was open, a gaping hole into a dark apartment. Tensed, he slid inside, ready for whatever might come. He grabbed for the first gun hanging on the wall – it was still there.

He unhooked it from the wall and flipped on the lights, ready to spray the room with bullets. No one was there. The apartment wasn't even ransacked. That made Junior nervous – maybe an old enemy had planted a bomb or just wanted to prove he or she could get into Junior's home. That's when he noticed the bathroom door – also gaping open.

He looked inside. There was water all over the place. Chachi was gone.

Junior threw down the gun and ran to Second Main Street. There was not a blond sailor to be seen.

Chachi was waking up with a headache for the second time in twenty-four hours. What he saw first was not the hold of the freighter he was in, or even the ropes that bound him to the floor, but nearly a dozen flax-haired sailors, gazing down at him with wide blue eyes.

"Behold. The Geek awakens," intoned one, and all twelve bowed, their golden heads dipping toward him.

Chachi, once again, began thrashing.

"Who the fuck are you? What the fuck am I doing here? Where the fuck am I? I am a fucking important fucking person and fucking Junior is going to have your fucking heads, you fucking fucks!"

All of the sailors seemed shocked.

"You cannot talk like that, your Geekiness," said one of them, stepping out of the way as Chachi aimed a kick at him. "You are sacred, most beloved of our god. You are the Geek."

"What the fuck did you just call me?" screeched Chachi, lunging at the sailor who had spoken.

"You are the Geek," said one sailor, looking a little surprised. "He," here they all solemnly high-fived, "is your Best Friend, and it is for you to make him chuckle, partake in his mischievous pranks and do his Holy Homework. Such language as yours is unbefitting."

"What the fuck is wrong with you?" Chachi exploded, launching into a stream of vitriol. "I have no fucking idea what the fuck you are fucking talking a-"

One of the sailors sighed.

"He must be silenced. The Principal will make him see."

All Chachi saw was one of them swinging at him, then a flash of red, then darkness.

Junior, armed to the teeth, was slogging through the foot of water on the First Tier, the exercise churning the breakfast in his belly. It was not even noon, and he was running toward the docks wrapped in several rounds of ammunition, with ten very chilly grenades clipped to his belt, a dagger hastily strapped to one thigh (it was beginning to chafe), two huge guns in his hands, several smaller ones strapped to his person, and a machete —which he hoped to hell was properly sheathed – slung over his back. A policeman had already asked him where he was going and Junior had simply told him that he was late for work. It was the truth. (The policeman looked at him judiciously and let him go on his way.) Junior had never been in such a hurry.

He was slightly nervous about what he was going to do once he reached the docks. He was pretty sure the ship could not have left already, but how to find the right ship.

He need not have worried. As he approached the docks, a large bright aquamarine and hot pink freighter was hastily being prepared for departure by hundreds of platinum-haired sailors. Junior, the large man draped in artillery, gaped at the fluorescent ship in horror.

The civilian blond man from the diner was arguing with a group of sailors at the gangplank to go aboard. Junior crept around the ship until he spotted another, less-trafficked gangplank. He made a beeline for it but stopped behind a crate when he saw three of the wholesome-yet-raffish sailors milling around it. He would never be able to get up to the ship with them standing there. He needed to get past them.

After a couple of seconds of careful thought, Junior stood up and walked right up to the group of young men. They smiled raffishly.

"Can't come aboard, Mack," said one, shaking his platinum mane.

"Yeah, Mack, sorry," said another.

"Me too," replied Junior and quickly shot all three astonished sailors in the head. Their handsome bodies splashed into the ocean. *Dead people*, he thought once again, as he jogged up the gangplank and onto the deck, *are much more manageable than live ones.* Junior was in luck – he quickly found a small storage room where he could hide out for as long as it took the ship to get where it was going. It wouldn't be pleasant – in fact he planned to be hungry, dirty, cold, bored and probably just as uninformed as he was about this Bay Side lab thing for the whole trip. His plan was basically to sit and wait, sleep and maybe forage for food if he got real hungry. He doubted anyone with any kind of information would happen to walk by, chatting about it while he was hiding.

He didn't harbor any fantasies about getting through the air vents either– he was a big man and air vents are usually made of flimsy metal that's suspended from the ceiling by even flimsier metal – they are, after all, meant to carry nothing heavier than air.

No, Junior just had to hunker down and wait the trip out. So, on the day he'd planned to sober up Chachi and plan his vacation, Junior found himself hiding out in a closet only slightly bigger than he was, willing himself to fall asleep for the whole trip.

Eight hours later, the ship nosed up against a dock in the middle of the ocean, at an island that rose conically from the water to a peak in the dark sky. On that peak was a large, one-floor building. If Junior were able to read, he would have seen that the large raised letters on the side of the building said Bay Side. What he did see, as he snuck off the ship (most of the sailors seemed to have been drawn into a fracas in another part of the ship), was a twisting dirt road reaching ever upwards toward the peak. Junior took advantage of the sailors' absence to piss on the side of the road, then readjusted his artillery and began jogging up the path.

Up in the Office, the Principal watched Junior's ascent with interest before picking up the intercom.

"We have an intruder," he said, slowly and deliberately. "See that he has an unobstructed path to the Library. Bring the Geek to the Auditorium."

By the size of the headache he had, Chachi was pretty sure he'd put up an impressive fight before he was knocked out for the third time. He woke up, dimly aware that he was being carried through the rain, several damp blond heads bobbling near his as they hauled him on their shoulders up the path to Bay Side Labs. He tried to smack one of the golden coifs but found he was hogtied. One of them turned to look at him as he struggled.

"We are sorry, your Geekiness," said the young man. "But there doesn't seem any other way to get you to Him."

Two of the sailors high-fived over Chachi, who started swearing only to realize he'd been gagged. This was not his day, he thought, looking up into the rainy, dark sky. The rain soaked him, and he closed his eyes and tried to forget where he was until he heard a click like a door being unlocked and opened his eyes in time to see the sky being replaced with a doorframe, then a red exit sign, then ceiling tiles. He watched the ceiling tiles move over him – he followed the tiles first in one direction and then another, until he was carried under another doorframe and into a room where the ceiling dropped away into darkness.

"We are at the Auditorium, as you told us," said one voice, then, to the other sailors: "Put down the Geek!"

Chachi found his world turning around and righting itself. As he was untied he saw that he was in a huge room filled with thousands of seats facing a large stage. On the stage were six platforms topped by six thrones.

Five of the chairs were empty. Chachi began struggling as he was forced into strange, ill-fitting clothing — a brightly colored button-down shirt with pictures of trees and half-naked women on it and a pair of clown-like pants, baggy around the legs and tight at the ankles — and propelled towards the front of the room. The person in the sixth chair on the stage watched him approach with drugged, sleepy interest. The sailors wrestled Chachi onto the stage and into a throne near the person, chaining him down.

Mopping a sweaty brow, a sailor bowed before Chachi and apologized for the rough treatment.

"The Principal will be here soon," he said and retreated into the darkness of the Auditorium.

"Nice fight, Mack," said the guy to Chachi's right.

Still gagged, Chachi glanced over at the guy. He looked just like all the sailors, only more so, somehow. He was chained but not gagged, and even though this guy was obviously under the influence of something, there was a mischievous sparkle in his eyes and a roguish twist to his smile.

Hm, Chachi found himself thinking as he looked into the azure eyes of his neighbor, *I'd do him.*

"I see you've been reunited with His Coolness," said a voice that echoed from the hidden ceiling and walls. "Welcome, Geek. I am the Principal."

Off in the darkness of the Auditorium, the unseen guards chanted, "You have a pal in the Principal."

The shadowy figure of a tubby, gray-haired man was emerging into the light. He stopped short when he saw Chachi and lowered his eyes.

"Good God," he whispered, "You look just like him."

Junior was surprised. At everything. There was no security at the door of the complex – in fact; he was able to walk right in. No alarms went off, although he was sure that several of the blond drones that occupied the building had seen him, trotting with his mobile armory through the halls. Junior traveled quickly, avoiding the halls with anyone in them, hoping he'd eventually find an open door that would let him start checking things out.

As if in answer to his prayers, he turned into a short hallway that ended in a pair of open double doors. Cautiously, Junior moved through them, into a dark room filled with moving lights. He found himself in a room full of lit screens, each showing re-runs of an ancient form of entertainment – the Television Show. Junior, like most people, had heard about such things as a child, but dismissed it as having nothing to do with his life and therefore, as being irrelevant. Confronted with the reality of this ancient artifact, he did what any average, working-class twenty-fifth century man would do – he stared.

On each screen, a drama unfolded, played out by six teenaged characters. One of the characters looked just like most of the people he had seen today. Another looked just like Chachi. Junior backed up a little to better see one of the televisions and nearly began firing wildly when he backed into something. It was a couch, and a very old one, by the look of it. Intrigued, Junior set aside his weaponry and sat down to watch.

"It is an honor to be in your presence," said the Principal, bowing in front of a skeptical Chachi. "I have spent my whole adult life trying to bring Coolness back to the planet; trying to resurrect the Six Paragons of Coolness: the Prom

King, the Prom Queen, the Football Captain, Student Council President, the Best Dressed and you, the Geek. "

"You are one of our gods," said The Principal, in response to a puzzled look from Chachi, He moved onto the stage, passed Chachi's throne and kneeled before the drugged being in the other throne. "And he is your Best Friend, the Prom King. Before him even you bow.

"Now," he said, producing a syringe, and inserting it into the god's arm. "I will awaken him and our quest for Coolness will begin!"

No sooner did the needle leave the young man's arm, than he began to slowly glow. Chachi started to edge away from the awakening god.

"Heya Mack," he said, looking over at Chachi with alarming charisma. "Wanna cut class?"

"Oh come on, you never cut class in your life," said a voice from the dark auditorium. Junior was standing in the aisle, automatic rifle in one hand, machete in the other.

I've seen your strange wholesome teen comedy," he called. "I know."

The guards tensed.

"We are prepared for you! Beware, we have been well-trained in fire drills," said one of the legions of golden young men menacingly.

"You have seen! You wish to join our movement, then?" asked the Principal. The god beamed rakishly and several guards fainted in delight.

Junior laughed and turned toward the stage.

"I have a little sister who's about your age," he said to the golden boy in the throne.

"Yeah?" asked the god, interested. "Is she cool? "

"She's hot," said Junior, advancing toward the stage slowly. "She's been knocked up twice already. You know what that means?"

The god's face seemed to lose some of its glow.

"It means she had sex – although really, she's been fucking since she was twelve so we shouldn't have been surprised."

"Don't do this," said The Principal, moving toward Junior. "He's not stabilized yet. He must only be exposed to coolness."

Junior put a bullet in his foot. The Principal howled in pain and Junior kept moving towards the stage.

"She must know that's not cool," said the god, casually breaking the golden chains, which held him to the throne, and standing. "It's cool to stay in school."

Junior laughed.

"Oh she didn't go to school," said Junior. "We kept my sister home to do hard labor. She never learned to read very well. Just enough to know the letters and numbers on my guns - you know, so she could help me sort my ammo."

The god staggered back into his chair.

"Guns don't kill people," he intoned, his voice strained, "People kill people."

Chachi was watching with wide eyes, working his mouth, trying to spit out his gag.

"And run drugs for the neighbors," continued Junior. "She was a really smart kid, my sister. She could drop off four bags of the good stuff, blow four clients and be home in time to get dinner ready for the rest of the family. Come to think of it, she probably would have done well in school, but then again, she might have been motivated by all those beatings."

The god's golden face was beginning to change, becoming less solid, more unstable.

"Just say no," he gasped in a strange, wild voice.

"Noo," wailed the Principal from the floor where he was crawling towards Junior. "Stop. It was my favorite show. I spent my life trying to do this!"

Junior shot the man in the shoulder. He fell to the floor sobbing.

"You know," said Junior, hoping his final words would push the rapidly degenerating god over the edge. "I don't think she would find you very cool at all. Maybe if you were on drugs or something."

But the final blow came from Chachi, who finally managed to spit out his gag.

"You're a dork," he said.

No one could have known that the golden boy would explode.

"You know, I feel kind of cool. Like by association," said Chachi, wiping some of the goo from his face after Junior released him.

"Piss off," said Junior, shooting the Principal in the head as the legions of wholesome young men sobbed at the doorway. "Let's just hope someone wanted one of these fools dead enough to pay for it."

In the lab, another vat begins to bubble. A slender, feminine hand reaches out of the vat, followed by a lovely, yet intense face.

"I must pass the SATs and get into college," she mutters. "And I must…. I must save the whales."

"Piss off," says a voice above her.

The face has just enough time to look shocked before a bullet is fired through the delicate flesh of her forehead.

"Let's go already," says another voice. "I was drunk all week, I've been knocked out three times, and I haven't eaten all week. I feel like crap."

"Keep complaining and you're next," says Junior, and bickering, the two voices retreat into the distance.

JOHNNY DEPP WEARS HEELS

~*~

Jill Bodach

Author's Notes: The inspiration from this story came from Greco, who wanted to be Benjamin Franklin and Drew who wanted Johnny Depp to be his drinking partner. The thought of Johnny Depp in heels was too good to pass up so I ran with it. And any story meant to feature Mitch Hedberg should offer some comic relief so it is my intense hope that you laugh out loud as you read. As for the last scene, please don't try this at home. If Johnny Depp himself should read this, I hope he is not offended.

~*~

Alex readjusted himself so he was sitting up a little straighter against the brick wall. He rested his guitar on his lap and stretched out his fingers in an exaggerated gesture that was meant to demonstrate to the people looking at him that he was a musician – a serious musician – who needed to first stretch his fingers before he could begin to play his instrument, and if they intended to listen they should perform some stretches of their own – stretch their minds perhaps – so they could wrap their brains around what he was about to play for them. And he would be taken seriously too – if he wasn't wearing a long, flowing blond wig.

That aside, just when Alex had settled in for a night of entertainment on the streets of Bridgeport, he heard a voice from above him say, "Hey, aren't you the cat who works here on Wednesdays and Saturdays?"

When Alex looked up to see who had spoken to him he was surprised to see Johnny Depp – not *Pirates of the Caribbean* Johnny Depp but *Edward Scissorhands* Johnny Depp with a little *Willy Wonka and the Chocolate Factory* Johnny Depp for good measure – staring back at him.

"What the fuck?"

Alex's brain was having trouble comprehending what he was seeing.

"I knew that was you man. Ha ha, you like the costume? I love Halloween."

Johnny Depp did not seem to think that there was a problem with his ensemble.

Alex was appalled. The man looked surprisingly like Johnny Depp except he was wearing bright red high-heeled shoes.

"What is up with the shoes bro? Johnny Depp doesn't wear heels."

Johnny Depp laughed.

"That's my own touch. I'm dressed up as Johnny Depp dressed up as Edward Scissorhands dressed up as a Ed Wood dressed up as Willy Wonka. It's a costume in a costume in a costume. And it's a conversation starter. It's crazy shit, right? Who are you? Axl Rose?"

Alex looked over at his recently discarded wig and shook his head again.

"No. I'm Fabio."

"Oh. Does Fabio play guitar?"

"No."

"Then why are you playing the guitar?"

Alex didn't really have an answer other than that it was his night off and he played guitar on his nights off and it was Halloween so he was dressed in the cheapest costume he had been able to find at the eleventh hour.

"Cuz I'm me dressed up as Fabio dressed up as me."

"Fucking awesome," Johnny replied and leaned over to tap Alex on the knuckles. "That's so fucking cool. See you inside man. Rock on."

Alex tapped knuckles back and watched Johnny being Edward being Ed being Willy.

"Fucking weirdo," he said.

With Axl Rose on his mind, Alex strummed the first few chords of "November Rain," a depressingly long song that should take an adequately long period of time to play, perhaps long enough that when Emily arrived it wouldn't appear that he was waiting for her.

He was just getting into it when he heard, "Alex, is that you man?"

Alex looked up to see the face of his friend, Michael, a.k.a Neil, a.k.a. Johnny Dakota, a.k.a George staring back at him from under a wig of grey unruly hair.

"Jesus H. Christ, Michael. Who the hell are you?"

Michael looked angry and pulled a light bulb out of his pocket and held it over his head.

"I have a brilliant idea," he said.

"Oh yeah," Alex replied. "What's that?"

"No douche bag. I'm giving you a clue."

"I hate clues."

"Wait, just one more. My idea is *electrifying*."

Alex pulled his blond hair into a ponytail.

"I'm not playing this game with you asshole."

"God, are you stupid? I'm Benjamin Fucking Franklin."

"That's the dumbest costume I've ever heard of. And besides Thomas Edison invented the light bulb, not Ben Franklin, you moron."

"Oh yeah? Who are you supposed to be? Axl Rose?"

"Fuck Axl Rose. I'm Fabio."

"I'd rather be Axl Rose. Much more heterosexual."

"Okay Benjamin Fucking Franklin. Think that guy got laid a lot?"

"Dude, he invented fucking electricity. Hell yeah he got laid. Wouldn't you want to lay the guy who invented fucking electricity? I would."

"I am not you."

"You comin' inside or you just going to strum your gee-tar out here all night long?"

"Was thinking of strumming my gee-tar. That alright with you?"

"Whatever. More ass for me."

Alex tossed up his hands. "The ass is yours for the taking."

Benjamin looked over both shoulders and then leaned in close to Alex as if he had something very important to tell to him and him alone.

"I heard that Emily might be here tonight."

Alex pretended not to care as he again resumed strumming his guitar, changing the song to one by Van Morrison as to deter any further Axl Rose comments.

"Don't act like you don't care."

"I'm not acting like I do or I don't."

"You might as well have just said, I know you are, but what am I? That is the most ridiculous thing I've ever heard."

"What do you want me to say?"

"What would you say if I told you I heard she was dressed as Jessica Rabbit?"

Alex continued to strum.

"Fine. Have it your way. I'll be inside…lighting the place up."

He walked away, chuckling at his own joke.

Alex did not laugh.

Emily. That was a name that ran through his mind at least fifty times a day, and at least ten of those times were followed by some alone time in the bathroom. It was inconvenient and not always a pleasant experience, but he couldn't help himself. It was just what she inspired in him. He had been after her for six months. It was a sad six months to be sure because his attempts were mediocre at best and usually resulted in her laughing at one of his poorly timed jokes while hitting his arm and saying, "Oh Alex." He had become her confidant and the pourer of her favorite drink, which also happened to be his favorite drink: Maker's Mark Bourbon on the rocks. He should have asked her out the first time she'd come into the bar but he had been too shy that time and the eight or so times that followed. After that, it had become that weird place where it's too late to say anything, like when you're in the car on the way home from dinner and you are still contemplating whether or not to tell the person you're with about the big piece of lettuce between her two front teeth.

Still, her name excited him in a way that nothing had since he saw Elizabeth Berkeley in *Show Girls*. It was too much to handle, particularly if she was dressed as Jessica Rabbit. He put his guitar back in the case, straightened his blond wig and stood up.

"If you can't beat 'em, join 'em," he said under his breath.

The inside of the bar was a cesspool of movie stars, politicians and mascots of various sports teams. There was even someone dressed as a donkey being led around by someone dressed as Shrek. Alex remembered why he hated Halloween.

He was an intellectual although his tattoos and often in-your-face approach led most people to think otherwise. He liked to read and was even pretty good at writing poetry. He was also good at sarcastic one-liners and could throw a person out of the bar and insult their intelligence all before they knew what had happened. He knew a lot about music, a little about politics and knew how to cook a pretty mean jambalaya. These were all things he thought might impress Emily, if he had the chance to share them with her. Instead all she knew was that he worked at the bar and played in a band on the weekends. A band that was not bad but wasn't going to go anywhere unless Alex spent more time writing music. Only he was scared to write music. What if people didn't like it?

He went to the bar and got right behind it; working or not, he didn't like it when anyone else poured his drink. Besides, the bar was like a second costume. He took on a different persona from back here and all his inhibitions, like the one that told him he was never going to be good enough for a girl like Emily, went away. Back here, he was comfortable and safe and had a certain degree of control over everyone else. He liked it. As he started to prepare his drink he was immediately assaulted with phrases like:

"Hey Axl. Where's the rest of your band?"

"Hey dude. Nice hair."

Alex ignored it all and poured his drink, careful to fill it to the right spot.

"The perfect pour."

Alex looked up and saw Emily dressed in sultry Jessica Rabbit perfection, complete with the tight red dress and, he guessed because he could not see them, red high heels, comparable to the ones worn by Johnny Depp.

"Hey Emily. Nice ensemble."

"Thanks. You too. Love the Fabio wig."

"You're actually the only one who's gotten that right," he said smiling.

"What? Really? It's obvious. People are dumb."

She pointed to his glass. "Can you pour one for me with those magic hands?"

If only you meant that, Alex thought.

"Anything for you, Jessica."

Emily made rabbit ears above her head and smiled.

"Thanks Fab."

I bet Fabio never had a problem asking a girl out. Hell, even Benjamin Franklin apparently got laid more than me. Maybe I need to invent something. He had once thought of developing a toilet seat that put itself down. This had been after an ex-girlfriend had made him pee outside after never remembering to return her toilet lid to the closed position he had found it in.

"Hey, who's dressed as Mitch Hedberg?" Emily asked.

Alex looked up across the bar and saw the distinctive sunglasses of his favorite comedian. He squinted.

"I have no idea. Pretty realistic costume though."

Emily took a small sip from her drink and started to walk away.

"Don't forget to have some fun tonight, Alex," she said.

He looked up at her and smiled.

I only wish you could help me with that, he thought.

Alex tucked his guitar case under the bar and thought about going out into the crowd but changed his mind.

Alex sipped his drink and thought about how the principles behind Halloween should be ones that people embraced all year long. People loved Halloween because it gave them the chance to be other people. Why didn't they just do what they could to be those other people all year long? Live like they were dying, Carpe diem and all that shit. He included himself in all of this. There was so much more he wanted out of his own life but he was usually too afraid to get it. That was why he couldn't ask Emily out. He didn't want to ask her out until he was the person he wanted to be. And he wasn't sure how long that was going to take.

"Hey man, I think Mitch Fucking Hedberg is here."

Alex's contemplation about life was interrupted, as it often was, by Junior. Alex didn't know his real name and never really thought to ask. The guy had been coming into the bar everyday for as long as Alex or anyone else there could remember. His favorite drink was rum and coke, *a boring drink*, Alex thought. Tonight Junior was dressed as Arnold Schwarzenegger in *The Terminator* movies but Junior, being Junior, looked more like Arnold circa *Kindergarten Cop*.

"Yeah, it's a great costume," Alex said, automatically refilling Junior's glass and hoping that would be all it took to get him to go away.

"No, man. I think it's really him. It sounds like him and everything. And he hasn't come out of character yet."

Alex wanted to say, "Mitch Hedberg is dead, you idiot. But instead he just shrugged and said, "Some people get really into Halloween."

"Who are you?" Junior asked. "You look like a male version of Barbie."

"I would have said Axl Rose," a voice from behind Junior said.

It was Thomas who was dressed as Ron Jeremy. Alex couldn't think of a more unlikely comparison to the 42-year-old man before him than Ron Jeremy. Even Thomas must have thought it was a stretch.

"And both of you would be wrong," Alex said.

Under his breath he muttered, "Fuckers."

"What do you want champ?" Alex asked Ron Jeremy.

"Anything on ice," he replied.

Fucker, Alex thought again.

"So did you see Emily?" Arnold Schwarzenegger asked as he drank his rum and coke. "She looks pretty foxy."

"She's a rabbit," Ron Jeremy said.

Alex wanted them to stop talking. About Emily. About Mitch Hedberg. About everything.

Alex methodically poured four shots of baby Guinness.

"Who's the fourth one for?" Arnold asked.

"Mitch. Can you bring it to him?"

"Sure thing man. Cheers."

Alex took the shot with Ron and Arnold and then watched as they walked the last one over to Mitch. He watched as Mitch took the shot, raised it in Alex's direction. Alex raised his hand.

Damn, he thought. *That really looks like Mitch Hedberg.* It made him sad that his favorite comedian was dead.

Alex spent the rest of the night pouring drinks for people he both liked and hated, drinks he knew would make them feel good and drinks he knew would make them sick tomorrow. He fielded more comments about Axl Rose and Mitch Hedberg, and counted the number of people dressed like someone from one of the Harry Potter movies. He kept a close eye on Johnny and Ron, realizing that they could be fodder for something he wrote later. His brother, Todd, had called last week and begged him to come to California.

"Dude, I never see you, and what do you have going for you out there?"

"My band. My job."

"Are you the fucking Goo Goo Dolls?" Todd had asked.

"What?"

"I said, are you the fucking Goo Goo Dolls?"

"No, we're not the…"

"Okay then. Unless you're the fucking Goo Goo Dolls don't stay in shitty Connecticut for a band. Next. Do you work at the Viper Room?"

"No I don't work at the Viper Room."

"Then come to fucking California man. There's ass out here."

The Viper Room. That reminded Alex of Johnny Depp. He peered over the edge of the bar and saw that the bright red heels were still on the feet of good 'ol Johnny. That's dedication, he thought.

Before it was even midnight, the official end of this silly holiday, Alex was ready to call it quits and go home. He was tired of being himself and tired of being himself being someone else when he heard, "Hey, what are you doing here?"

Alex was refilling his already half-empty bourbon when he saw Xena, the Warrior Princess approaching. It took him a minute to figure out it was really Kate, the proprietor of the bar.

"Everyone is taking this Halloween thing way too far," he said.

"It's Halloween, honey. The night when things are supposed to be taken way too far while we're dressed as other people so we don't feel as embarrassed the next day."

"I guess."

"That's the only way I can explain what just happened to me," she said sliding her empty glass across the bar.

Without even having to ask, Alex began filling it with Absolute Citron.

"What happened?" he asked.

Kate leaned across the bar and exposed way more of her warrior princess self than Alex was prepared to see.

"Lean closer. I don't want anyone else to hear."

Alex leaned in closer and so did Johnny Depp although it was clear that he was pretending not to listen but he had lowered his drink and was staring straight ahead of him.

"Emily just tried to kiss me."

Alex lost his grip on the Absolute bottle and it went crashing to the floor.

"Jesus Christ, Alex!"

"Jesus Christ what? You just told me that Emily tried to…"

"Keep your voice down!"

Alex angrily wiped at the spilled vodka. Some of it had gotten in his hair. He thought about just taking the wig off and mopping the liquor up with that but decided against it.

"Our Emily is a lesbian," Ron Jeremy said. At some point during the conversation he had joined them.

"Apparently," Kate said as she adjusted her shield.

"No way," Alex said. "She can't be. There's no way."

"Of course there is a way Axl," Ron Jeremy said with a grin. "Do you want us to explain it to you?"

"By the way," Johnny Depp interrupted. "Is that really Mitch Hedberg over there? No one seems to know who that guy is."

"No you idiot. Mitch Hedberg is dead. As a fucking doornail."

He turned back to Kate. "I mean, there's a way. Of course. But Emily? She's too…too…"

"Too sexy?" Kate offered. "You need to get out of the mentality that all lesbians are butch. What's the woman who was with Ellen Degeneres?

"Anne Heche," Johnny Depp offered, taking a slow sip of his Corona.

"Yeah. Her. She was the most delicate lesbian I'd ever seen."

"But isn't she really straight?" Ron Jeremy asked.

"I don't know. Is she?" Kate pondered.

Alex fumed. How could they be making pop culture references at a time like this? He went back through all of his conversations with Emily. She had mentioned other men, hadn't she? He thought back and realized that while she had talked about men, she had never actually talked about them as something she was interested in. Usually the conversations were about how distasteful it had been when someone was hitting on her or how awful it was to get cat calls while she was out jogging. Had he missed all the signs? The theme from *The Crying Game* started to play in his head.

"I gotta get outta here," he said. "Sorry about spilling the vodka Kate. See you Wednesday."

"Hey! Where are you going? They haven't even given out the prize for best costume yet."

"You can tell me about it Wednesday. I'll be back then. I gotta go now."

He came out from behind the bar and gave Kate a quick kiss on the cheek.

"Sexy costume. Hope you win."

"Bye Alex. Take care of yourself."

"I will."

He reached back around the bar for his guitar case and headed for the door.

"Mind if I come?"

It was Johnny Depp. Alex didn't really want anyone to come let alone Johnny Depp but he didn't have the energy to argue.

"Sure. Let's go."

Alex had driven his car to the bar but he felt like walking for awhile so he put his guitar in the backseat and headed down the road. Johnny Depp followed.

"You liked Emily didn't you?" Ron Jeremy asked. "You know what always helps me?"

"What?" Alex turned around and, at first, he didn't see Johnny anymore. "Where the fuck…"

He looked down and Johnny was lying on the side of the road.

"What the…"

"I know it looks strange but you should try it."

"Try what? You're going to get killed man."

"That's what I mean."

"What? You mean I should try to get killed?"

"No, I mean you should lay here for a minute. C'mon. Just do it."

Alex felt like he was back in grade school and a classmate was challenging him to run up behind the teacher and put a "kick me" sign on her back. Alex had gone to Catholic school so not only would an act like that have been frowned upon but it would have also held the promise of extra Hail Mary's, Our Father's and, of course, the threat of the eternal damnation of his soul.

Whatever.

A car whizzed by and Alex was sure that Ron was going to lose a body part, at the very least a finger, as his arms were spread out to his sides like he was making an asphalt angel.

Johnny sat partially up so that his head was no longer against the pavement.

"Alex. Lay down. Don't you trust me?"

"Actually, no. I don't. I hardly know you."

"Then I have no reason to lie to you."

Alex knew this was faulty logic but again found himself lacking the energy to argue. He lay down on the pavement in front of Ron, his feet nearly touching the other man's.

"So what am I supposed to be feeling exactly?"

"As if at any moment, your life could be squashed out of you by the wheel of a pickup truck."

"That's fucking great."

"No, seriously. Think about it. From down here, everything that matters when you're vertical doesn't matter anymore. Like that girl…what's her name?"

"Emily."

"Emily. It doesn't matter that she's a lesbian. You have bigger things to worry about."

"Like being squashed by a tractor trailer?"

"Precisely!"

Strangely, Alex thought he was starting to understand.

"You do this a lot?" he asked Johnny.

"At least once or twice a week."

"Ever get caught?"

"Once. The cops took me to the hospital. They thought I was suicidal."

Alex understood how they could think this.

"But no other times?"

"Nope. Most times people just think I'm crazy. Or drunk. Or already dead. It's the great thing about living in America, this part of it anyway. It's the only place in the world where people are relieved to think you might already be dead. That way they don't have to try and save your life or waste their time calling an ambulance or something."

This Alex understood as well.

He thought about all the time he had spent thinking about Emily. It was time he could have spent writing music. He now knew that Emily had not spent time thinking about him.

"I hear ya. It's like no one cares about anyone else anymore," he said.

"Yep," Johnny said. "But when you're down here you realize that you are actually more insignificant than you think you are. I mean, why should people care about me? They have their own lives and problems."

"Which are also insignificant!" Alex said, finally truly understanding. "They just don't realize it."

"Exactly bro. Exactly."

"When you're down here," Alex continued. "No one matters more than anyone else. We're all small. Everyone matters as little as everyone else."

"I dig it man," Johnny said. "The way you see things."

Alex was beginning to dig the way he saw things too.

Just then, a car passed by and Alex sat partway up to look at it and a familiar head of dirty blond, greasy hair in the driver's seat. An arm fell out of the window in a half wave as it went by.

"Thanks for the drink man," the person behind the hand called.

"Dude, I think that really looks like Mitch Hedberg," Alex said.

"See, man. What did I tell you? Things just look better from down here."

Alex, whose head was being cushioned by his blond Fabio wig, had to agree.

Alex settled in. He was no longer scared about being run over. Instead he focused on the street light and tried to count the number of moths swirling around it. He'd never noticed that before. He'd been too busy. He felt like he was on some sort of drug-induced trip. He liked it. Suddenly Emily seemed very far away and somewhat comical in her Jessica Rabbit costume.

He smiled.

He even liked Johnny Depp's red high heels.

And he didn't even mind if the people driving by thought he was Axl Rose.

AFTER HOURS

~*~

Marissa Benning

Author's Notes: The inspiration from this story came from Arianna. While it isn't as explicit as she might have liked (or as I had originally wrote it), I hope it fuels a few fantasies for her.

~*~

Arianna watched Lexie from the far side of the bar as she downed the last of her drink before requesting another Velvet Vagina. She tipped the tattooed bartender generously before taking her drink and seating herself on the corner of one of the couches were she could watch Lexie, who was talking animatedly with some of the regulars, unnoticed.

She sighed and tucked a stray piece of her long, curly hair behind her ear, wishing it was Lexie's graceful hand doing so. She didn't know when she developed a crush on the bar owner, only she wouldn't call it a crush really, more like a deep, unfulfilled lusting. She wanted Lexie, wanted to feel her blonde hair brush against her skin, feel those lips on hers. She shook her head and tore her eyes away from Alexandria and refocused on the guys playing pool in the back.

She had to stop thinking of Lexie this way. It was useless; Lexie was straight and not interested in fulfilling Arianna's fantasies. It was time to move on. Arianna recrossed her legs, feeling slightly self-conscious in her too-short skirt. She wore it because she knew, that when paired with the right heels, it gave the illusion that her legs went on forever. Her great body was an asset that she knew how to use to its full potential. Unfortunately, she was realizing that her efforts tonight were for naught. Oh she caught the eye of many of the men in the room, but the ones she wanted to rake over her barely gave her a glance.

Sighing, she swirled her cup and knocked back the last of its contents. *Well,* she thought, *if I am not going to get laid, I might as well get drunk.* She gave a sly smile to one of the men eyeing her from the bar. Sure enough, he arrived at her side two minutes later with another drink. She may not want to sleep with men, but that didn't mean she'd turn down free drinks from them. *Might as well put my beauty efforts to work for something tonight,* she mused, almost feeling sorry for the poor guy, knowing no matter how many drinks he bought her, he would still be going home alone.

Jeff, he told her, was a teacher at one of the local private schools. She tried not to yawn as he rambled on about children and their delicate young minds. *Breeders!* When Jeff excused himself to use the loo, she nearly made a run for the exit, but was stopped when Matt arrived with another drink and a shot, courtesy of the bartender.

"Drew said you looked like you could use this," Matt said, handing her a Baby Guinness.

She saluted Drew with the shot before downing it, licking her lips. "That's definitely one of his better inventions," she said.

"Yeah, sure beats that strawberry, orange, lime thing they were mixing up the other night," Matt agreed. "So why aren't you over talking to Lexie?"

"It's pointless," she answered with a shrug. "I've decided to just get drunk instead and go home alone."

"Getting drunk. Well that's something I can help you with."

By the time Jeff returned, three of Matt's friends had joined them on the couch. In an effort to cheer up Arianna and liven up the night, Matt suggested they play a drinking version of the Moods game that was lying around.

Two hours later, the six of them were far removed from sober. The bar had nearly emptied so that just Lexie, two of the regulars, and they remained.

"I haven't been out this late in years," said Jeff, yawning. "I should be heading home. Can I give you a lift?"

"No thanks," said Arianna. "I'm going to stay and sober up awhile before driving home."

Matt and his friends left twenty minutes later, leaving a still-tipsy Arianna alone on the couch with ten minutes until last call. As Drew closed the bar, Lexie motioned for Arianna to stay seated. "You are too wasted to drive anywhere," she called across the bar.

Arianna tried to protest but realized Lexie was correct. So instead, she settled back onto the couch and closed her eyes, enjoying that comforting feeling a buzz brought.

When she opened her eyes, all the lights were off except the Christmas icicles that decorated the silent room. Drew had apparently gone; the closed sign was anchored firmly on the door. She thought it odd that Lexie hadn't kicked her out. Wondering where Lexie was, she got up to investigate.

She found her in the back room slowly rolling the cue ball back and forth over the green felt of the pool table.

"You seemed like you were having a good time with the boys tonight," she said in a way that made it sound like a question more than an observation.

Arianna thought about it for a moment. "I did," she answered.

"You certainly were laughing a lot. Jeff and Mark couldn't keep their eyes off of you," Lexie remarked.

"Really?" Arianna replied in an uninterested tone.

"I am surprised you didn't go home with one of them."

"Why would I do that?" Arianna asked, genuinely surprised.

"They are both handsome, good guys who seem to think the world of you."

"Lexie, I am a lesbian," Arianna pointed out, wondering just how much Lexie had to drink tonight.

"Are you?" she asked as if looking for confirmation.

"Is that a problem?"

"No, not at all. In fact…"

Arianna cocked her head and stared at the other woman whose voice went silent and whose eyes were locked on the white ball rolling across the felt. "In fact what?" she prompted.

Lexie slowly raised her eyes and met Arianna's curious gaze. Arianna was surprised at the look of desire she saw reflected in them. Trapped under the intensity of that stare, she didn't move as Lexie sauntered over to her.

Lexie reached out and gently tucked an errant lock of hair behind Arianna's ear before gently skimming her fingertips along Arianna's cheek. Arianna leaned into the touch. Feeling brave, she turned her head and placed a gentle kiss on Lexie's palm.

As if that were some hidden signal, Lexie's hand threaded into Arianna's hair and pulled her head down so that their lips met. Lexie took advantage of Arianna's surprised gasp to allow her tongue to slip into the other woman's mouth.

The intensity and passion of the kiss caused Arianna to moan in delight as her arms snaked around Lexie, pulling her body flush with her own. This had been what she had been waiting for. She didn't know what had brought on this change in Lexie, and she didn't care to know. Even if it was just for now, just for tonight, she intended to take advantage of the situation, regardless of what tomorrow might bring. Her hands stroked Lexie's back as Lexie's fingers tangled in Arianna's curls, their tongues fighting for dominance.

Lexie broke the kiss to explore the soft skin of Arianna's neck. Tossing her head back, Arianna exposed her throat to Lexie's hungry mouth which converged over her pulse point eliciting a groan from Arianna, whose hands threaded through blonde hair, pulling Lexie closer.

Arianna had wanted this for so long; she couldn't believe she was finally experiencing Lexie's soft lips on her skin. She knew in that moment, she would do whatever Lexie asked as long she kept kissing her. Dragging Lexie's mouth to her own, Arianna poured her desire into her kiss as she hungrily tasted Lexie, her tongue exploring the contours of that sweet mouth.

When the kiss ended, both were breathing heavily, standing close enough to feel each other's body heat but not touching. Arianna raised a shaking hand and lightly skimmed Lexie's bare arm. "Are you sure?" she asked, her eyes trained on her fingers.

Lexie raised Arianna's gaze to her own.

"Yes," she answered before claiming her mouth once again.

When their breathing returned to normal, Arianna raised up on her elbows to take in the flush still coloring Lexie's cheeks as she lay back on the felt.

"You're beautiful," Arianna said, tracing Lexie's kiss-swollen lip.

Lexie smiled against Arianna's fingers before capturing her wrist and placing a chaste kiss on her palm then lowering it. "This wasn't exactly what I was intending to happen tonight," she said, gesturing to the pool table the two reclined on, their clothing strewn about.

"Do you regret it?"

Lexie held Arianna's face between her hands, locking their eyes. "Not one minute of it."

Arianna's reply was lost in the certainty of Lexie's kiss.

SANDRA'S JOURNEY

~*~

Erika K. Zamek

Author's Notes: This story was inspired by the butt-kicking bar mistress who wished to be immortalized as a butt-kicking warrior princess. Like any warrior woman worthy of her sword (or staff), her character came to me as strong, vulnerable, and intelligent—exactly the sort that I strive to bring to life. I had intended to tell her tale simply as a quest chock full of action and excitement, but the moment Justin stepped onto the page my mind started to whisper...what is a medieval adventure without a little romance? And so this fable was born...

~*~

Sister Sandra lounged behind the bar, contemplating the boisterous crowd filling her tavern and silently thanking the sky for the rain that had been beating against the windows since late afternoon. The warm, bright pub was a haven from the first traces of winter, and those who had taken refuge danced and laughed to lively melodies spun by bards she'd bribed away from her longtime rival and sparring partner. Adam owned the establishment a stone's throw down the road, and he routinely swung between attempting to steal her customers and scheming to draw her into marriage. Five years of trying had not earned him success in either venture.

She sipped the bitter citrus liquor brought earlier that day by a trader from across the sea, savoring the tart flavor and smiling over the goblet as one of her serving wenches liberated a healthy sum from a table full of merchants. Most of her patrons preferred ale or mead, but perhaps the exotic spirit would bring her a more sophisticated crowd—and their coin. Her coffers had benefited from the weather, which meant that she could soon leave the tavern in the capable hands of her staff and escape into an adventure that would satiate her hunger for something outside the ordinary.

She was startled from her thoughts when a man took the barstool before her, brushing water from midnight hair and leather sleeves. He appeared young, perhaps near her age, but his serene blue gaze and weathered look hinted that he'd not led a sheltered life. Her instincts whispered that he could give her what she desired.

"What can I get you?"

His eyes swept over her long blonde plait and worn leather bodice before coming to rest on the chalice she'd set down on the shelf behind her. "I'll take some of whatever you have in the goblet back there. I presume that it is more interesting than what the rest of this throng is drinking."

"Excellent choice," she replied as she retrieved a second cup and poured a generous measure of the spirit. He sipped the clear liquor, rolling it across his tongue before nodding in appreciation. "Exceptional. Where did you find it? I've traveled much of the world and have not tasted anything like this."

"Have you? Are you a soldier?"

He laughed, eyes twinkling with amusement. "That is one way of looking at it, I suppose. I am a warrior for hire. I go where my whim takes me and serve those who need my skills."

Sandra smiled and leaned against the shelf at her back, picking up her goblet and taking another sip. "What sort of places have you visited?"

She was not disappointed as he entertained her with tales of his travels, occasionally chiming in with an anecdote from her own experiences. The need to serve other customers occasionally drew her away, but he was always waiting for her return with the same warm smile. The crowd had started to thin when she finally allowed the conversation to focus on her.

"So what do they call you?"

"Sister Sandra," she said, offering him her hand. "You?"

"You don't look like a servant of God to me," he replied with raised eyebrows, giving her fingers a gentle squeeze.

She chuckled. "Hardly. We are a family here, and I refuse to be called 'mother'." And you are?"

"Justin."

The sound of a throat clearing next to her reminded Sandra that she was still holding his hand—and that they were not alone. The rest of the bar had faded away as they talked. She let go of his strong fingers before turning toward the interruption.

Maeve, her head serving wench, was watching them, a mischievous grin lighting up her heart-shaped face. "We're nearly out of mead."

"So open another cask; we've plenty downstairs."

"I need your help. Tristian is too busy to carry it up, Dorian is breaking up a fight in the corner, and Nate is off in the back with Anna taking a break."

"What about Ben?"

"He went home an hour ago—sick."

"Might I be of some assistance?" Justin asked, glancing over at Maeve. "You're needed up here; the goblets shouldn't be allowed to run dry, after all."

Sandra hesitated a moment before nodding. "I'll take him down."

Maeve bowed her head in acknowledgment and returned to the floor, but not before shooting a knowing smile at her. Sandra rolled her eyes before leading Justin to the back stairs and down to where they stored the tavern's beverages and food. The mead casks were lined up along two of the walls, and she gestured to the one closest to the stairway. She tried to help, but he waved her off. He was about to lift the barrel when a commotion from the floor above captured her attention.

"Wait here a moment," she told him, moving to the steps and pulling a dagger from her bodice as she ascended. He didn't listen very well, for she immediately felt his presence behind her and the pressure of his blade against her arm.

The sound of screaming and clanging metal grew louder as they emerged from the stairwell. Sandra started to run forward, but Justin held her back. She rounded to demand that he let go of her, but he didn't give her the chance.

"You can't help anyone caught up in it. Be cautious."

Concern for the people she loved warred with the logic driving his words, but she knew that he was right. She nodded, and he released her. They crept quickly to the partially open door at the end of the hall and peered into the now-silent room. Bile rose into her throat as she took in the tableau.

Stone-faced soldiers had most of the patrons and staff trapped on one side of the room, murderous gazes as effective as the scarlet-streaked blades they held in cutting down thoughts of rebellion. The bards were already silenced, their blood dripping off the stage, painting trails of crimson on the uneven stone floor. A lump rose in her throat when she recognized a few of her regulars lying prone around the cadre, sword hilts lying in outstretched limp hands.

One of the invaders had forced Maeve to her knees and was holding a dagger against her throat, a look of gleeful anticipation etched across his face. Sandra could see her hands shaking, but her eyes shone with defiance. A dark-haired man clad in black leather paced before her, sword gleaming at his waist and hands clasped loosely behind his back. "I ask you again. Where is the Princess Cassandra?"

"I know no one by that name."

The soldier pressed the blade harder against her neck, drawing a thin line of blood from the alabaster skin. Sandra's eyes widened, breath freezing in her lungs.

"You're lying. My search led me here, and I am never wrong. Where is she?" His smooth, confident baritone enthralled the imprisoned crowd, and a seed of fear took root in Sandra's heart when several pairs of eyes flickered toward the door behind which she hid.

Maeve remained silent, and the soldier wrenched her head back, stretching her throat taut. The action broke Sandra's paralysis. She was reaching for the handle when Justin's hand closed around her arm and he dragged her away from the door. She struggled against him, breaking free and running toward the opening. He again seized her and hauled her down the hall, pinning her against the wall so hard the stones dug painfully into her back. She winced, but he didn't step away, probably didn't even notice. He was staring intently at the sliver of light spilling through from the room beyond, as if waiting for soldiers to burst through at any moment and discover their presence. The ominous tones of the leader's voice were the only thing that reached them.

"Let me go!" she hissed, fighting to escape Justin's hold. She failed; his body was like wiry steel.

"Are you trying to get yourself killed, Cassandra?" He asked, finally turning back to her.

She fell still, studying him warily. "What are you talking about?"

"I saw your face when he spoke that name. You are who he wants."

"No, I'm not."

"Yes, you are. Don't bother to deny it; I can see the truth in your eyes."

Sandra fought the urge to look away, instead forcing herself to meet his gaze with a defiant stare. "I'd rather he take me than hurt Maeve."

"He'll kill you."

"You don't know that," she argued, but there wasn't much strength behind it. Her instincts agreed with him.

"Trust me...he will."

A wail from the other room drew them both back to the door. She bristled when he kept an arm locked around her.

Maeve was still kneeling before the same soldier, but Dorian lay dying on the floor in front of her. Tears streamed down her cheeks as the light faded from his eyes.

Sandra choked back a sob. Maeve and Dorian had been planning to wed in a few weeks' time.

"Now then...I ask you for the final time. Where is the Princess Cassandra?"

Maeve was staring at Dorian's body, her face a mask of rage. "Go to hell," she spat, glaring up at her questioner.

He turned toward the door that hid Sandra and Justin, chiseled features painted in boredom as he gestured over his shoulder to the soldier holding her. Maeve's brief scream of pain filled the room as the young man drew the dagger across the side of her neck. Someone moaned as blood spurted from the wound, scarlet splash staining Dorian's tunic. The leader brushed invisible lint from his shoulder before turning back to the crowd cowering not far from where her body had fallen.

Sandra's cry was muffled by Justin's hand over her mouth. He dragged her back down the hallway. She didn't resist him this time.

"We need to get you out of here."

She didn't answer. The dagger hung at her side, fingers loosely curled around the hilt. The door to the bar filled her vision, Maeve's murder playing across the grainy surface. The woman had been like her sister; the last person she'd been that close to had died in her arms. The sensible part of her insisted that it should be easier this time, but that rationalization did nothing to shatter the paralyzing shock that held her prisoner.

"Sandra! Listen to me," he whispered, forcing her to look at him. His features swam in to partial focus, fingers warm against her skin. "We need to get you out of here. Does this place have a back door?"

His urgency cut through the fog enshrouding her thoughts and she pointed down the hallway to a door at the very end, opposite the one leading back into the tavern. He nodded and guided her toward it, stopping to listen for several moments before turning the handle. He frowned and glanced back at her.

"How many are out there?" she asked, grooved steel of the dagger's hilt digging into her palm as she tightened her grip.

Surprise flickered across his features. "Four."

She bit her lip. "My staff is upstairs—"

"We don't have the luxury of going to get it," he interrupted.

She glared at him, embracing her anger and praying that it would keep her alive. "Fine. Two for you and two for me. Don't get in my way." Without waiting for a response, she opened the door and dove out, narrowly avoiding the blade of a barrel-chested man with a face so scarred she could barely make out his features.

Sandra heard Justin curse as she rolled back to her feet and faced the men that stalked toward her, barely visible in the swath of dim light that escaped the hallway. A sword shined in the hand of one, while a dagger flickered in the fingers of the other. She swallowed hard, scanning the barely-cleared land around her in search of an advantage. The cold rain drenched her hair and clothing within seconds, and a smile crept across her face as the stream running between her shoulder blades gave her an idea.

"If you want me, come and get me," she taunted, easing into the darkness of the stand of trees at her back. The man with the sword charged forward, shoving aside bushes and saplings as he pursued her. She ghosted silently to an ancient oak that lay just ahead and pressed her body against the gnarled bark, listening to his crashing footsteps and tensing when his annoyed grunts drew close enough that she could feel his breath when his head swung toward where she stood. The rain masked the burble of the rocky stream flowing by two steps from the tips of her boots, and when he ambled just ahead of her hiding spot she crouched and slashed his hamstring. He yelped in pain, but before he could round on her she slipped out onto the path behind him and gave him a shove forward, sending him tumbling into the water with a splash.

When she was confident that he wouldn't rise again soon enough to trouble them, Sandra crept back along the path to edge of the clearing, her steps stilled by the scene that greeted her. Justin had engaged the three remaining men, moving like a whirlwind with a face of ruthless determination. None of their blades did more than leave the occasional scar on the leather he wore like a second skin. He embodied the skill and grace most she knew strived to approach, and it was all she could do not to stand there mesmerized by his fluid motions.

Giving her head a shake, she tightened her grip on the dagger entered the clearing, hoping to take one of them down before they realized that she'd returned. She'd almost reached where they fought when the soldier wielding a dagger spotted her and slithered away from the others. He wasted no time in seeking her blood, striking out in an arc across her body. She danced back, tip of his blade passing a hairsbreadth from her chest. When he lashed out again she blocked and spun away, leaving a deep slash on his arm as she went. He hissed in pain and glared at her, clapping a hand over the bleeding cut.

She stalked closer to him, taking in the blood coating his fingers as he sneered at her and lunged. Instead of leaping back she sidestepped the attack and darted forward, sinking her dagger into his side. His face contorted in shock as he fell, and she was grateful that he didn't cry out.

Sandra whirled at the clang of steel meeting steel close enough to ring her ears, and her eyes widened at the sight of Justin and the remaining soldier with blades crossed a whisper from her throat. She dropped to the ground, nearly landing on the man she'd just stabbed.

"Don't move," Justin barked, fierce glare never leaving his opponent. She gripped her weapon more tightly and looked for a way to help him. His shoulders shook with the strain of holding back the other man's sword, but it was nothing compared to the shudders that wracked his foe's arms as the man struggled to best him. Without warning, Justin twitched his blade upward and the soldier fell forward, tripping over where she lay on the ground and falling on top of the one that she'd defeated. His weapon sailed into a bed of dying flowers along the wall of the tavern. Before she could move, Justin spun his sword between his palms, and with a small smile of triumph plunged it into the back of the man he'd felled.

She watched him apprehensively as he gave his blade a twist before pulling it free, scrambling back and rising as he wiped away the blood using the soldier's sleeve. He was watching at the still-open door into the bar as if expecting more soldiers to emerge. When none appeared, he finally looked over at her.

"Are you hurt?"

Sandra shook her head, surprised by the concern in his voice. All traces of malice were gone from his face and the brutal light had vanished from his eyes. It was as if he'd shed an unpleasant mask.

He closed the door as quietly as the rusty hinges would allow and pulled her around the side of the building, pausing at the entrance to the main street.

"Stay here," he ordered, brushing water out of his eyes.

She leaned against the weathered wood and returned the dagger to her bodice, excess vigor starting to fade and burning tears forming behind her eyes. She forced them away. Not yet. When I'm safe. When Maeve's death will mean something.

He returned a few moments later guiding a sleek black stallion. She crossed her arms, studying him carefully as he held out a hand her.

"Why?" She asked.

"Because you need my help."

"I can't pay you. Everything that I have is above the bar."

"Don't think about that now. Come on. We need to leave this place."

"How do I know that I can trust you?"

He sighed, exasperated. "If you couldn't trust me, I'd have let you sacrifice yourself or simply stood by and watched that soldier kill you."

Sandra still didn't move, looking over her shoulder at the pacing shadow beyond the windows.

"We don't have time for this. We need to go. Now." He paused, and continued in a gentler tone. "I'm not going to hurt you...that I promise."

She hesitated only a moment longer before taking his hand and allowing him to pull her up before him on the stallion's back. He reached around her and took the reins, signaling the horse to move. Sandra didn't know where they were going, but his strength at her back was reassuring.

Countless shadowed buildings passed before he drew the animal to a halt before a three-story stone structure with warm light pouring from nearly every window. He tethered the horse before leading her into the building and through the tavern to the stairs at the back. Like her own, this establishment was packed to bursting with rowdy people seeking to escape the weather.

The crowed jostled her as she followed him through, each blow shattering a piece of the wall her anger had raised around the shock and guilt at what she'd caused. By the time they reached other side, the barrier was gone. The rickety stairs creaked under her feet as she trailed him up to the third floor, and their footsteps echoed in the blessedly empty hallway as he lead her to a corner room.

She stood just inside the door, clutching convulsively at her sleeves as he lit lanterns and candles, steadier light diminishing the shadows cast by the crackling fire. The furnishings were simple but looked comfortable. There was only one bed on the wall to the right of the door, but it was a large one, and the sofa sitting just off the foot was lined with gently worn cushions that begged her to sit. The low oak table in front of the couch shined in the glow of the hearth, as did the desk on the wall opposite the door. The only signs that he had actually spent any time here were the battered saddlebags leaning against the bottom drawer and a worn book lying on the desktop.

"Stay here. I'll be back soon."

She nodded, not looking at him. Once he'd closed the door and locked it behind him, she lay her dagger down on the desk and walked over to the bath. A porcelain basin nestled in an iron stand sat against the far wall, and a round mirror hung just above it. A green towel dangled from a peg to the right of the sink. Sandra rested her hands on the cool white bowl and peered into the mostly-clean mirror. The rain had washed away the muddy evidence of the skirmish, but she barely recognized the red eyes that stared back at her. Maeve's smiling visage appeared in the glass, laughter ringing in her memory. The image faded when she heard Justin calling for her from the main room.

"Here," he said, offering her a bundle of ivory material. She unrolled it and was surprised when it took the form of a nightgown.

"Where did you get this?"

"Don't be concerned about it. Just go change and get dry."

Too tired to argue, she nodded in thanks and returned to the bathroom. Her hair was still dripping wet, so she unraveled the braid and dragged her fingers through the unruly strands, drying it as best she could with the towel before shedding her wet clothes and hanging them next to the towel. The nightgown was soft against her skin and left her shoulders and part of her back bare to the cool air. When she emerged, he had changed into a loose tunic and pants and was hanging his own wet garments over the desk chair.

"Better?" he asked.

"Yes, thank you."

"It was nothing," he told her, fiddling with one of the leather bands encircling his wrists.

The awkward moment was broken by a knock on the door. He opened it and stepped out for a moment, returning with a tray piled high with roast meat, vegetables, and bread. A jug of wine and two goblets were nestled between the plates. Sandra's stomach growled when the enticing aroma reached her. She hadn't realized that she was hungry.

He set the tray on the table in front of the couch and sat, gesturing for her to join him. When she'd settled into the cushions that were as comfortable as they looked, he asked her the question she'd been dreading since he'd deduced her secret.

"So why are Lord Dolomon's soldiers looking for you, Princess Cassandra?"

She stared into the fire, shock starting to dissolve in its warmth. "I am a Princess no longer. My family disowned me when I was thirteen. Who is Lord Dolomon?"

"Why?"

Sandra sighed. She hated it when people ignored her questions. "I refused to play the role of the obedient princess that my father wanted. I have three sisters, all of whom he used to gain alliances or land. I chose to create my own path rather than be used to further his."

He nodded, chewing thoughtfully.

She tried again. "How do you know who those soldiers worked for?"

"I've tangled with Dolomon's men before. A nasty lot, to say the least; it wouldn't surprise me if they killed half the people in the bar trying to find you."

Sandra stared down at her lap, stilling fingers that twisted the ivory fabric, determined to keep her emotions under control. "Why would he be looking for me?"

"I was hoping that you could answer that question."

She shook her head. "I have no idea."

"You've had no dealings with him in the past?"

"None. When I left home, I traveled around for a time to see all the places I had read about as a child. When it was time to settle, I ended up here."

Justin eyed the dagger glinting in the firelight. "What did you do during your travels?"

She hesitated, but his open expression convinced her that she should be truthful. He'd already seen her fight and was probably wondering where she learned how. "I moved about with a soldier who left my father's service at the same time. He was a bit like you, actually. At first I just acted as his healer and would periodically earn money for us by treating others. He taught me to fight with the staff and dagger, and when he felt I was ready, I started to get more involved in the other aspects of his work."

She took a swig of wine, the liquid burning a path down her throat. Justin was watching her curiously.

"What happened to him?"

Sandra peered down into her goblet, as if expecting a different answer than the one she had to give to appear in the liquid's smooth surface. It struck her after a moment how much the deep red liquor resembled blood and she set the cup down with shaking hands, nearly sloshing the contents onto the table. "After a few years of moving around, we'd gathered enough gold to be selective about the assignments we accepted. He was fascinated with the lore and mythology of the places that we visited, and had started searching out legends and treasures to pursue. There are plenty of wealthy nobles that sponsor that sort of quest. The glory is irresistible."

She paused, pulling her knees up to her chin and gazing into the leaping flames. "Our last quest involved searching out a rare gem thought to have been lost a hundred years ago. Legends are funny, though; as they are passed down, the quality or powers associated with the articles they surround tend to be glorified with each retelling. We did find the jewel, but the noble who sponsored the hunt believed that we were cheating him, passing off an inferior substitute for the original. The lord had his food poisoned that night…there was nothing that I could do."

"I'm sorry."

Sandra nodded in thanks, keeping her eyes trained on the fire. "He taught me never to live an ordinary life. To honor his memory, I never have and I never will."

"What was his name?"

She smiled. "Bryan. His name was Bryan."

"Something tells me that Bryan would not have wanted you to give yourself to Dolomon."

"He wouldn't have. He would have done exactly what you did. But…Maeve and Dorian and everyone else in that pub are my family. The first I've had since I lost him."

"They died to protect you. That is what families do—even adopted ones."

She closed her eyes, quelling the desire to rail against their deaths. "What could this Dolomon possibly want with me?"

"Did you and Bryan ever work for him?"

"Not that I can recall."

Justin paused, mulling over the possibilities. "When was the last time you had contact with your blood family?"

"The day I left ten years ago."

He frowned.

"What....you think this has something to do with them?"

"Yes, I do...we should speak with them."

"What do you mean that we should speak with them? I can't ask you to accompany me. You know I have no money."

He stared at her, eyes filled with something powerful and unclear. Bryan used to look at her that way.

"Dolomon's man likely had watchers in the tavern all evening. It is how he knew that you were there."

Sandra sighed, remembering the time they spent talking. Anyone looking for her would need to be blind not to have noticed.

"My fate is now linked with yours," he finished, setting his plate on the tray.

"I'm sorry," she said quietly, staring at her half-finished meal on the table.

He reached out and laid a hand against her cheek, forcing her to look over at him. "It is what I do."

"But I—"

"There is no need to worry about payment."

"But—"

"I would be on the same path regardless of whether you were with me or not, simply because I spoke with you. We will solve this mystery together."

She nodded, placing her plate on top of his on the tray. Rising, he took it to the hallway and left it on the floor next to the door. She was reaching for the bedcovers when he next spoke.

"What happened to your back?"

She faced him. "What do you mean?"

"Where did these scratches come from?" he turned her around and swept her hair to one side, tracing his fingers over her upper back and shoulders. The gentle touch stung, and she was again struck by how such violence and tenderness could live side by side within the same person.

"Probably from the wall in the tavern...the edges of the stones aren't sanded down in the hallways."

"I'm sorry that I hurt you," he murmured, leaving her for moment to dig through one of his saddlebags.

"I'm fine. It's nothing that won't heal in a day or so."

"Even so, this will help," he replied, pulling a small bottle out of the bag. A spicy herbal aroma wafted from the container as he twisted off the lid and started applying the mixture to the scrapes. Her skin tingled, and she wasn't sure if it was because of the salve or because of him. Sandra stifled a yawn and chalked the feelings up to exhaustion.

"Take the bed," he told her, re-sealing the container and returning it to his bag.

"Where will you sleep? The couch isn't nearly long enough."

"It will do."

"The bed is big for both of us. Just stay on your side," she told him, peeling back the covers and sliding between them. The sheets weren't silk, but they felt nearly as soft as she pulled the blankets up to her shoulders and sank into the soft mattress. He climbed into the other side after extinguishing all of the flames except those in the hearth.

"Try to sleep," he said softly. "You're going to need the rest."

Sandra didn't answer. Whenever she closed her eyes, all that she saw was Maeve's body tumbling to the ground, landing with her head on Dorian's chest.

When Sandra awoke, she was alone. Rubbing sleep from her eyes, she sat up and scanned the room. Justin's saddlebags rested against the desk and the clothes he'd worn the previous night were still draped over the chair; he hadn't continued on without her.

She rose and dressed, leaving the nightgown neatly folded on the end of the bed. Retrieving her dagger from the desk, she stared at the intricately etched blade that had been a gift from Dorian the pervious year. His eyes had been bright when he'd handed her the carefully wrapped bundle, his voice reverent as he'd described its journey through his ancestors. Stories told by his father and grandfather had convinced him that it had special powers, and since his skill lay more with the sword than the dagger he'd wanted her to benefit from its mystical qualities. She rested the cool metal against her forehead and vowed to use it to avenge his death. And Maeve's.

She curled up on the window seat and stared out, watching as loaded wagons lumbered by, narrowly missing scruffy children that darted and played in the street while their parents haggled with aproned shopkeepers. Bryan had hustled them out of places without warning before, usually because rival seekers were jealous of their success…but none of those villages had been a home to her; they'd never had real friends, put down any sort of roots. Despite her periodic travels, she had planted her hopes for a future here, and the thought of ripping them out so abruptly left a dull ache in her stomach.

She caught a glimpse of Justin's dark hair in the crowd, and he slipped through the door not long after, carrying a long staff and a leather pack.

"Good, you're awake."

"Why didn't you rouse me earlier?" she asked, not moving from the window.

"You spent half the night tossing and screaming with nightmares. I thought the sleep would do you some good."

She blushed. She had awoken several times to find him holding her or stroking her hair in an effort to calm her. It had been a surprise, but she hadn't stopped him.

"I'm sorry if I kept you up," she murmured, turning back to the bustling street.

Silence stretched between them before he finally spoke. "You'll need these," he said, only briefly glancing at her as he held out the staff and pack.

She slipped off the sill and walked over to him, taking the weapon from his grasp. It was the right height for her, and was made of a strong yet flexible wood. The finely-hewn shaft felt smooth and she gave it a spin, pleased when no stabs of pain from splinters pierced her hands.

"This is a superior weapon," she said, stopping the rotation and holding it still.

"I thought so. My skill with one is merely moderate, but the man I spoke with assured me that it would serve well."

"It will. I've not used one of this quality. I look forward to testing it out."

"Hopefully you won't have to."

"We may be in this together, but you have your agenda and I have mine. The man that killed Maeve and Dorian will pay."

"Killing him won't bring them back," he murmured, watching her with that same unreadable look. "It may not bring you the closure that you crave."

She didn't answer. Resting the staff against the bed, she held out her hand for the pack, which he reluctantly handed her. The leather was of good quality and it would hold anything that she may need it to.

"Thank you."

A muscle in his jaw twitched as if he wanted to say something, but he let the subject drop. "You're welcome. I spoke to the innkeeper; he said that Dolomon's men were here early this morning asking questions. We need to leave."

"Did anyone reveal that we were here?"

"No. But it is safest not to stay. You can ride, I assume?"

"Of course."

"Good."

He packed his belongings, and they left the inn. A delicate mare frisked beside his black stallion, seemingly eager to run free in the crisp air. Sandra smiled wistfully, wishing that her own motivations could be as simple. Justin turned to her once she was settled on the mare's back.

"So where are we going?"

She paused, stroking the horse's mane. "Alexandria."

"You're the heir to Alexandria?"

"I was one of them. Why?"

"I worked with your father several years ago, helped him train an elite group of soldiers. He suspected that a neighboring kingdom was preparing to attempt a takeover, as he had no living successor."

She frowned. "He has three other daughters. One of their children will take the throne."

Justin shifted in his saddle. "Sandra, one of your sisters died in childbirth, and neither of the others has been able to carry a baby to term. Your family has no direct heir to Alexandria save you and your children."

She stared down at the horse's mane, eyes starting to burn with tears at the loss of her sister. She'd had no idea that her family had fallen onto such hard times. She closed her eyes briefly, suppressing the rising sorrow. She couldn't allow herself to freeze up as she had the previous night. There would be time to grieve later.

"Come on," he said, eyeing something over her shoulder. "Dolomon's soldiers may still be in the area. He kicked the stallion to a gallop, and the mare immediately followed suit at her light touch. So he knows how to choose horses, too. Like Bryan. Sandra barely knew Justin, but something about him made her feel as if she'd come home.

Alexandria was over a week's ride west of them, but the time passed quickly. They spent most nights in inns, sharing a large bed with an invisible line down the middle that neither crossed intentionally, though several times she did wake from nightmares of Dorian's sightless eyes to Justin's soothing touch and voice. He never mentioned it, and neither did she.

Their fifth day of riding brought them to a secluded clearing in the mountains, no towns in close proximity. Twilight fell as she set their bedrolls in a sheltered area hugged by the roots of massive trees that stretched toward the clouds. He built a small fire, and they sat quietly eating smoked beef, bread, and cheese obtained in the last town.

When the last of the crumbs had been brushed to the ground, he handed her a mug of tea that had been steeping at the edge of the flames and returned to his seat across the fire. She took a sip of the steaming liquid, smiling as the soothing chamomile slid down her throat. She'd been increasingly more nervous as they approached her homeland. His news on her family had been running through her mind since they'd left that first morning, stirring to life an unexpected curiosity about fulfilling the responsibilities she'd abandoned. She found it ironic that one of the things that had driven her to run so many years ago was part of what drew her back now. She doubted that her parents would greet her with open arms despite the circumstances of her return.

"We should reach Bayside in another two or three days," he said casually, taking a sip from his own cup.

"Yes."

The stallion grunted, trying to pull free of the branch he was tethered to.

"What should we do when we arrive? This is your family, after all."

She wrapped both hands around the mug and peered into the tea's glossy surface. She really had no idea what sort of reception they'd receive. "Probably take a room at an inn and seek out my father during the general audience."

He nodded. The mare whinnied nervously. Sandra set down her mug and turned to where the horses were tied. Both were pawing the ground, trying to get loose. Justin was watching her curiously, but he too had set down his cup and was listening to their surroundings. It was quiet. Unnaturally quiet. All of the usual sounds that accompanied a night in the woods were absent.

"We're not alone," she murmured, rising from the rock, gathering their beds and lashing them to the horses' backs. Justin's face was shadowed by the flickering firelight, but she could feel his tension. He retrieved her staff from the tree she'd set it against and moved to where she stood next to the mare. His breath caressed her skin as he spoke.

"I don't think that we have time for that," he whispered, pressing the slim wood into her hand.

He was right. A moment later, men in Dolomon's colors streamed into the clearing from all directions, surrounding them. Justin drew his sword and regarded her solemnly. "Time to dance."

He whirled, positioning himself at her back as the ring of soldiers started to close in. She twirled the staff expertly, and the men coming at her hesitated a moment before continuing. She smiled and lost herself to the rhythm of the spinning wood, the sound of steel on steel ringing through the night, and the feel of the staff impacting limbs and weapons as the soldiers attacked.

At first, they approached her mockingly, assuming that she had no skill with the weapon she held. They realized the error quickly when the first few to engage her retreated with cracked skulls and broken bones. The next wave fought with more skill if not caution, and she felt warm blood flow down her arms where their swords flashed through the spiraling barrier. It was only after she'd decimated the second and third groups that they began to approach more carefully. Despite efforts to draw him away, Justin's presence at her back did not waver.

The onslaught of soldiers appeared endless, and during a brief lull Sandra caught sight of man that had ordered Maeve's death standing just inside the ring of trees surrounding their clearing. He was studying them with a calculating look on his face, and she had the fleeting impression that he was watching her every move. A piece of her screamed to go after him, but she was not about to leave Justin unguarded. So she stayed where she was and prayed with everything she could spare that he would join the fray and she would get a shot at him.

Her plea went unanswered. He called back the group currently attacking her and gestured to someone off to his left. A brawny man bearing a staff moved forward, a dangerous smile on his face. She quashed her blossoming doubts and engaged him, parrying his strikes with relative ease. He was good, but she was better…or at least she thought she was better. It was starting to become a struggle to keep the staff moving, requiring nearly all of her concentration. The woods at the edge of her vision were fading in and out of focus like the sand beneath shallow waves. She was tired, more tired than she should have been.

Her opening came when he stumbled over a rock and his staff faltered in its nearly impenetrable speed. She seized the opportunity and poured her remaining strength into an attack, hitting his head and both hands in quick succession. He dropped his weapon and staggered backward, and she immediately hooked the wood behind his knees and took them out from under him. He crashed to the ground and lay motionless, blood trickling from the back of his head.

"Back!"

The deep voice matched that which had questioned Maeve, and Sandra watched as the ring of soldiers limped back to the woods with much more sound than they'd arrived with. She leaned against Justin but kept her staff ready lest they return.

"Next time, Princess," the voice promised, dripping with arrogance. She watched as he strode from the clearing and led his remaining men into the blackness of the night. They stood, panting, waiting for the next attack, but it never came. Perhaps he felt that she and Justin had bloodied enough of his men and did not want to lose any more. Their retreat did not make any sense, but she was too tired to question it.

She stumbled back, dizzy, as Justin took a step away, barely catching herself before she landed on one of the motionless soldiers littering the ground around them.

"Are you all right?" he asked, ignoring his own injuries as his gaze traced the blood on her arms.

"I'm fine."

He stepped forward when she staggered. She planted the end of the staff in the ground for support. "I'm just a bit worn out."

"You're bleeding pretty heavily…" He sounded worried.

"I'm fine, it's just a few scratches," she replied, swaying again, lightheaded. Her vision had begun to blur, and the right side of her neck felt hot and was stinging. She raised a hand to probe the area, and was shocked to find a slash along her throat. Blood seeped between her fingers. "I…I think that I need a bandage…" Her knees buckled as the woods started to spin around her in a haphazard kaleidoscope of leaping shadows.

He was at her side before she fell, one hand against her neck tightly covering the cut and the other around her waist and holding her upright. "Stay with me…"

He guided her back over to the still-crackling fire and lowered her to the rock, pulling her up when she tried to lay down. Keeping one hand over the slash, he rooted through one of his saddlebags with the other.

"Tired…" she murmured, swaying backward. He drew her back upright.

"I know that you're tired. You need to stay awake."

"Can't…"

"Yes, you can," he told her, pressing something firmly against the wound.

She winced but the pain drew her away from the hazy abyss, at least for a moment. He was rifling through the bag again, and a moment later she felt him pushing her hair aside and wrapping something securely around her neck.

She moaned when he tied off the bandage over the cut. "Sleep…"

"Not yet," he said, supporting her with one arm while he swirled some sort of powder into the tea mug that had miraculously not been knocked over during the melee and raised it to her lips. As the bitter lukewarm liquid slid down her throat, she remembered doing these very things for Bryan when he'd been hurt like this during one of their quests. She hadn't let him sleep, either.

"I need you to sit up on your own for a minute. Can you do that?"

His voice was uneven and faint, as if traveling to her across a vast distance. Sandra nodded, still fighting the dizziness. He left her on the rock and returned a few moments later with their bedrolls, laying them out next to the fire. He helped her to the ground and settled behind her, one hand resting on her stomach.

"I want you to focus on my voice…don't go to sleep. Just listen and answer."

She nodded and tried to do as he asked. She wasn't entirely successful, and he needed to shake her awake periodically. But each time he did his words sounded clearer, as if he'd closed more of the gap that lay between them.

He told her more about his adventures, the men he'd trained for others and the armies that he'd helped lead. She and Bryan had worked for some of the same lords, and Justin sounded pleased to compare experiences. Or he was pleased that she was still awake.

"How are you feeling? Are you still dizzy?"

"Not as much as before," she murmured, relieved when the clearing didn't start spinning when she opened her eyes.

"I think that it is probably safe to let you sleep now, then."

She nodded and started to slide off of him, but he wrapped his arms around her waist, holding her in place. "I'd feel better if you let me monitor your breathing for a while."

Too tired to argue with him, she shifted so that her head was resting more comfortably against his chest. He reached over and draped a blanket over them. The beating of his heart and the warmth from the covers lulled her to sleep within minutes.

When Sandra woke the next morning, she was curled up in the blankets alone. Her dizziness had subsided, but she still felt drained. She traced the bandage encircling her neck, shivering at how close she'd come to dying the previous night. He had saved her life.

"How are you feeling this morning?"

She sat up as he approached, noting the dark smudges under his eyes and the drag in his steps. "Better, but weak. I don't think that I could face another ambush like that so soon."

"Can you ride?"

"I think so."

"Good. I want to get through the mountains today. If Dolomon's forces are still out here, I don't want to be an easy target for them."

She nodded. "I'd just like to get cleaned up and change before we get going." The chemise that she wore was stiff with dried blood and most of her exposed skin was streaked in it. He'd bought her a second one in the last town they'd stayed in, and she was grateful to have something clean to put on under her bodice and skirt.

"There is a lake through those trees," he said, gesturing the direction from which he had come. "I didn't see any evidence of watchers, but be careful."

She nodded and rose, picking up her pack. *A bath will feel nice, even if it is a quick one.* She'd started to move in the direction he'd indicated when she stopped abruptly, looking around the clearing. "What happened to Dolomon's men?"

"Once I was satisfied that you were going to make it through the night, I moved them."

"Where to?"

"A dry streambed through the trees," he said, pointing in direction opposite the lake. "The ones that regain consciousness will find their way home. The ones that don't will be buried by the winter snow."

Sandra narrowed her eyes at him. "How did you find it in the dark?"

He hesitated, that intense look coalescing in his eyes again. "Go get cleaned up. We have a long ride ahead of us," he told her, strapping his saddlebags to the stallion.

She watched him for a moment before heading through the trees to the lake.

The sparkling waters were nestled in a valley between several jagged peaks that thrust up to the sky, a light coating of snow already visible. The air was cool but the water was just warm enough to immerse herself in, a balm to her tired muscles. She scrubbed her skin and hair clean before simply closing her eyes and floating in place for a little while, ignoring the throbbing in her neck that intensified as the slash was submerged; it wasn't the ocean that she'd frolicked in as a child, but it soothed her just the same. She had begun to rise and wade to shore to dry off and dress when Justin appeared at the treeline.

"Everything okay?" he called.

She immediately sank to her neck in the quiescent water, wincing at the sting. "Fine...I was just about to come out."

"Ah...okay...I'll just...go."

She smiled at his discomfort, pleased to have ruffled his collected exterior even if it was just a little.

She joined him a short while later, surprised to find that he'd packed everything, including the bloody chemise she'd left on the beach.

"Ready?"

"Yes," she replied, squeezing the last of the lake from her hair and trying to push the ache in her neck out of her mind.

He set a quick pace, and just past nightfall they reached a moderately-sized town barely through the mountains. Sandra tensed as they rode in by the light of the nearly full moon. She recognized this place as one she'd toured with her father when she was ten. They'd reached Alexandria.

Justin chose an inn on the far side of town that was set back from the main street. A quiet conversation and a few silver coins pressed into the innkeeper's palm earned them a large room and a guarantee that their presence would be hidden from any that came asking after them.

Once Justin had left to gather information from patrons in the tavern below, she pulled the bloody chemise from his saddlebag and tried to rinse out the stains, mesmerized by the pink water swirling in the porcelain bowl. The housekeeper had brought her several jugs' worth, but it wasn't enough to wash the fabric clean. She sighed and let the material fall into the sink.

Looking up, she caught sight of the pale strip of fabric wrapped around her neck in the mirror hanging on the wall above the basin. They'd stopped mid-day and he'd changed the bandage, spreading the same tingling salve across the wound that he'd used on her back the first night. It had eased the throbbing a bit, but the pain had returned by mid-afternoon and escalated to downright uncomfortable by the time they'd reached the inn.

Untying the tight knot, she unwound the material and gingerly peeled back the thick pad covering the slash, grimacing as cool air assaulted the torn skin. A bit of blood welled from the cut, but not enough to cause alarm. She'd been right that morning; if it had been much deeper, Justin wouldn't have been able to help her.

She replaced the bandage and retied the length of fabric. There was no need to change it, since he'd already done so before heading down to the tavern. She marveled at his dedication to keeping her safe, but didn't dare question it too deeply.

She hung the stained chemise to dry from a peg on the wall and dumped the last of the bloody water out the window before returning to the main room to examine the map he'd obtained from the innkeeper. She frowned as she traced the outline of Alexandria with a fingernail. When she'd left, her father's kingdom had stretched from the northern coast to the southern and encompassed all of the land between the eastern mountains and the western shore. Now it looked as if his reign only extended halfway to the southern coast. The word "Dolomon" was scratched in the parcel bordering Alexandria to the south. Justin had been right. Dolomon wanted the rest of her father's land.

But…the only way that killing her would achieve that would be if the rest of her family was already dead. Her stomach twisted into a knot. She hadn't spoken to anyone in her family since they'd disowned her, but somehow believing that they were alive and safe had been a salve to her guilt at refusing to conform to their wishes for her. The thought that they may be dead cracked her resolve that her choice had been the right one.

The room suddenly felt too small for her, as if the walls were closing in. The bright light from the lanterns they'd lit hurt her eyes, and the braid she'd woven that morning was giving her a headache. Sandra untied the string binding her hair and shook her head, releasing it into tight waves. She picked up the spare key and several silver coins, tucked them inside her belt pouch, and descended the stairs to the tavern.

She spotted Justin sitting at a table with a couple of men and several attractive women, one of which who seemed to have taken a liking to him. He didn't appear to be encouraging her, but he wasn't exactly discouraging her, either. A hollow feeling settled in Sandra's stomach when the woman laid a hand on his arm and whispered something in his ear. He smiled at her, and Sandra turned away and headed for an empty stool at the bar when the woman moved closer to him.

"What can I get you?"

The barkeep was a burly man with quick smile and kind eyes, and she immediately liked him.

"Whatever you have that is unusual," she said, returning his smile and forcing the image of Justin out of her mind.

His smile widened as he pulled a glass flask from behind him and poured her a tumbler of clear liquid. She picked up the glass and swirled the contents before taking a sip. It was the same exotic citrus liquor that she'd been drinking the night her life was sent spiraling onto this new path. Downing the drink in one long swallow, she gestured for him to pour her another. She started to feel flushed and lightheaded as the potent spirit pooled in her empty stomach and resolved to slow down a bit.

A steady stream of spirited songs flowed from the musicians performing at the front of the room, and a number of the more inebriated patrons had cleared a dance floor near the stage and were twirling about it, laughing and happy. She caught sight of Justin dancing with the same woman, leaning close to listen to whatever she was saying. Sandra turned back to her now-full glass and took a slightly larger sip than she'd intended.

"You're going to need to drink faster than that if I'm to buy you the next."

Sandra turned to see a man with soulful brown eyes and wild blonde hair standing next to her, watching her appreciatively. Perhaps the distraction would be good for her.

"I suppose you'll just need to wait until I'm done. I don't drink fast for anyone," she tossed back, giving him a smile.

His full lips curled upward in return, and he leaned on the bar next to her. The barkeep shot him a suspicious glance, but didn't say anything. Sandra made small talk with him as she slowly sipped the bitter drink and learned that he was a local merchant who sold high-quality weapons and armor. When he asked what she did, she kept her answer vague, revealing only that she was passing through. He frowned, obviously disappointed, and moved closer to her.

"We could go somewhere more private, away from the crowds." Something in his tone didn't sit right with her and the lightheaded feeling vanished. She grabbed the hand that was reaching for her arm.

"I don't think so."

"Is everything all right over here?" The barkeep had returned to her station, a fiery glare directed at her would-be suitor.

"Everything is fine. He was just leaving."

The man scowled at them both and slunk away. She relaxed slightly as he disappeared into the crowd.

"Are you all right?" the barkeep asked her, topping off her tumbler and placing a glass of water next to it.

"I am. Thank you."

"You're welcome. If you need anything, let me know."

She nodded and smiled as he bowed his head and returned to tending other customers.

"Good thing you got rid of him. He's got a reputation for accosting any beautiful woman that walks through that door."

Sandra turned to see a woman with long, curly hair standing close next to her, delicate features set in a sympathetic expression. "No worse then any other drunken lout you'd meet. Have you had dealings with him?"

"He's propositioned me several times, but he isn't my type. Doesn't like to take no for an answer; I've actually been forced to bloody his nose several times."

Sandra laughed out loud and held out her hand. "I'm Sandra."

"Arianna," she replied, accepting the offered hand.

"Pleasure." Sandra released her after a moment and gestured to the recently vacated bar stool next to her. "Care to join me?"

Arianna's face lit up into a brilliant smile. "I'd love to."

The bartender returned and brought Arianna a drink which she downed quickly, immediately gesturing for another. A woman after my own heart, Sandra thought idly as Arianna took a small sip from the newly-filled glass.

"So what brings you here?"

Sandra was again vague with her answer, but instead of asking for more details Arianna simply accepted her desire for secrecy and didn't pry. The musicians had started to play more loudly to be heard over a particularly boisterous group that had just walked into the bar, and they were forced to lean close to talk.

"So are you local?" Sandra asked her, taking another sip of the tart liquid. The lightheaded feeling was returning, and she realized that she'd better get something to eat before she fell off the barstool.

As if realizing how Sandra felt, Arianna turned to the barkeep before answering the question. "Anything left from dinner, Jake?"

"I'll bring you whatever we've got," he said, smiling at them. Sandra nodded in thanks, and Jake disappeared though a swinging door behind the bar.

"I am one of the local healers."

"One of them?"

Arianna's voice dropped to a more conspiratorial tone. "I am the only one who will heal the, shall we say, less-than-honorable citizens."

Sandra smiled at her. She liked the sound of that.

Jake returned before she could respond, two heaping platefuls of food balanced on his arm. Sandra's mouth watered at the heavenly aroma wafting from the roasted chicken, vegetables, and biscuits that he set before her.

They dug in, exchanging colorful experiences from their respective professions. Arianna had her shaking with laughter with a tale about a soldier who couldn't bear to have a sword wound stitched back together and had forced Arianna to chase him around the room with the needled and thread. Sandra returned the favor with a vignette about one of her patrons that used to strip down to his undergarments and sing, usually from a tabletop, when he'd had too much to drink. It usually took her and Maeve together to get the man dressed and home again.

Her laugher faded when she thought of Maeve. Arianna noticed, and pulled the stool slightly closer so that she wouldn't need to speak as loudly.

"Did something happen to Maeve?"

Sandra hesitated, finishing the last bite of chicken. "She was...she died in an accident. It was...a shock."

The look on Arianna's face clearly said that she didn't believe that was all there was to the story, but she didn't pry for details.

"Recently?"

Sandra nodded, laying her fork down on the plate. She was about to ask about Arianna's most interesting "less-than-honorable" client when the other woman pulled her into a comforting hug, stroking her hair the way that Justin did to soothe away her nightmares. Surprised, she hugged Arianna back, only pulling away when a throat cleared beside them.

Justin stood there, expression stormy. "I thought that you were still upstairs."

"I needed to get out for a while. You looked busy, so I decided to sit here at the bar," she said, a defensive note creeping into her voice.

"You should be resting."

"I'm fine."

"You aren't fine, you almost died last night." He picked up her glass and took a sip, frowning as he set it down so hard that a bit of the liquor sloshed over the rim. "Drinking is not what you should be doing."

"I'll leave you to it," Arianna said suddenly, rising from the stool.

Ignoring Justin for a moment, Sandra rose too and touched Arianna's arm. The other woman looked back at her.

"Thanks...it was a pleasure to meet you."

"Likewise," Arianna responded, covering Sandra's hand and giving a squeeze. Sandra released her, and Arianna vanished into the sea of people pressing in on them.

"What was that about?" Justin asked suspiciously.

Sandra spun to face him before resettling herself on the stool. He looked angrier than he had when he'd first appeared.

"What was what about? She took a seat, we ate something, and talked for a time. It isn't like I've had someone fawning all over me for the past two hours."

His face paled but he didn't answer. Sandra flushed, embarrassed by her outburst, and finished her drink in a single swig. She shakily set the tumbler back on the bar and slipped off the barstool, body mere inches from his. "Thanks, Jake," she called to the bartender, leaving the silver she'd brought next to her empty glass. He inclined his head in acknowledgment and returned to serving his customers.

She took a step away and stumbled. Despite the food, the strong liquor still affected her. Justin's arm was around her in a moment, steadying her, pulling her close. She felt as if someone had set the sliver of air between them on fire.

She stared up at him, ensnared by his intense gaze, skin tingling where his knuckles skimmed her cheek as he brushed a lock of hair from her eyes. He leaned in toward her...If I just...she shivered and stepped out of his embrace, determined to regain control.

"I'm going to go up now. I'm sure your table is waiting for you." She bolted from the bar before he could respond, climbing the stairs without too much trouble and berating herself for her words. It didn't matter what he did or with whom. He may be helping her, but it didn't mean that she had any claim on him.

Pulling the door shut and locking it, Sandra leaned against the heavy wood and closed her eyes. No, he definitely did not belong to her, but that didn't stop some part of her from wishing that he did. Sometimes she wondered if he might have similar feelings, or if she was just another job to him. She shook her head and pushed the thoughts from her mind. Head starting to ache, she shed her bodice and skirt and changed into the nightgown that she'd pulled from her pack before leaving the room. The alcohol was making her drowsy despite the steady throb in her neck, and sleep took her within moments of resting her head on the pillow.

When she awoke the next morning he was still asleep next to her, but in the night he'd again crossed the invisible line and it wasn't because she was screaming in her sleep. He was simply holding her tightly against him, breath warm against her neck. She gently lifted his arm, careful not to wake him, and slipped out of the bed. He mumbled, rolling into the space she'd occupied and burying his face in the pillow.

The housekeeper had left the wash water outside the door, which she lugged to the bathroom. When she emerged clean and dressed he was sitting up, hair tousled but eyes alert. Her fingers itched to rake through the wavy locks.

"Why didn't you wake me?"

"I figured that you needed the rest."

He frowned. "Why?"

"God knows how long you stayed awake to make sure I kept breathing the other night. I thought that you must be tired."

The frown melted. "Thanks."

She nodded in response and walked over to the map on the table. He joined her, standing close enough that she could feel his body heat against her shoulder.

"We are here," she told him, indicating a small dot in the foothills of the northern range. "We are going here," she continued, dragging her finger on a diagonal path to Bayside, the kingdom's capital on the coast. "It is a solid two days' ride to the southwest, but there is a town halfway in between that we should be able to reach by nightfall or just after."

"Then we should get going," he said, retrieving clean clothes from his saddlebag and walking over to the bath to get changed.

"Yes," she said quietly, staring at the map.

He stopped at her back and gently rested a hand on her shoulder. "I won't let anyone hurt you. That includes Dolomon or your own family."

She grasped his fingers and squeezed in response, feeling his gaze burn into the back of her head as he lingered for a few moments before slipping his hand out from under hers and continuing to the bathroom, door closing behind him with a soft click.

"I only hope that I still have a family for you to protect me from," she whispered to herself, rolling up the map and sliding it into the leather protective cylinder the innkeeper had given them.

When he emerged, she'd packed all of her things and most of his. He insisted on checking her neck again, and she had a hard time looking him in the eyes as he rubbed more of the tingling salve into the slash and rewrapped the bandage.

The ride to the next town did take the rest of the day, and they reached it when the stars were burning brightly overhead. It surprised her that he didn't visit the tavern that evening as he had in every other town that they'd stayed in, instead arranging for dinner to be brought to the room. Neither spoke of the words they'd exchanged the previous night or what had nearly happened in the bar.

His focus turned inward as he sipped at the last of the wine that had accompanied their meal, and Sandra took advantage of his distraction and went to bed early, telling herself that it was because she was still a bit drained and not because she didn't know how to handle the intensity of his gaze whenever he looked at her.

Unfortunately the sleep she sought was elusive, driven back by the sound of his quill scratching across parchment and her own rampant thoughts. Her curiosity about ruling had grown into a powerful wish to see her family's control of Alexandria restored. The startling desire had her tossing about until the faint light dancing along her closed eyelids finally vanished and she felt him join her, feigning sleep as he pulled her close. Rest did not evade her for long after that.

The next day they covered the final distance to Bayside, reaching the city near dusk. The sun floated above an ocean that beckoned her even from the high cliffs overlooking the city on which they stood. If she closed her eyes she could almost smell the tangy air of her childhood home.

"Are you ready?" his voice was hesitant.

"Yes. We should try to reach an inn before nightfall. Bayside is a popular location to visit, and I'd prefer not to sleep in the woods."

Justin didn't answer, just nudged his horse onto the trail that crisscrossed the cliff face until it reached the valley below. Sandra followed after one last look at the crashing surf.

Less than an hour later, she was tethering both horses at a mid-sized inn right on the water. Sailing vessels were docked nearby, passengers streaming onto land and making their way to nearby inns or waiting carriages. Justin's stallion nuzzled her hand as she loosened the bridle. They'd pushed the animals hard the past few days, but now they would have a chance to rest.

He had not returned yet from procuring them a room when she finished with the horses, so Sandra wandered over to a rail that overlooked the sea, enjoying the last of the sunset and relishing the feel of the salt spray against her face. She'd loved to play at the ocean as a child and had not been back here since leaving all those years ago. They'd spent time on the coast far to the east, but it wasn't the same. She'd missed this. The feeling was unexpected, and she wasn't quite sure how to handle it.

She resisted the urge to walk down to the beach and wade into the surf. Perhaps tomorrow, she thought, wrapping her arms around herself. The sun was sinking below the horizon in a spectacular riot of color when Justin joined her.

"You missed this," he observed, and she cursed his perceptiveness.

"Yes, I did. Some things have no substitute."

He nodded. "We got the last room in the inn. I nearly had to fight someone for it."

She smiled at the mirth sparkling in his eyes. "Thank you."

"You're welcome. Shall we?"

She nodded and they made their way along the rail toward the whitewashed building, sidestepping people that were milling about and avoiding the glares of those who had not been lucky enough to procure rooms. He bypassed the stairs and the tavern and led her to what looked like a dining room. Wood and glass glimmered in the candlelight as couples and groups ate and danced to the soothing music floating from string players on a dais at the front of the room. A woman in a crisp violet dress led them to a table near one of the many windows overlooking the sea.

She returned with wine once they were settled, filling their goblets before departing and leaving the flagon on the table. Sandra took a small sip, savoring the smooth texture and distinct flavors bursting to life on her tongue.

A serving woman approached and recited the menu for the evening. Sandra ordered something absently, distracted by the candlelight reflecting off of her wineglass as she slowly spun it between her fingers. Justin's voice drew her back to the present.

"So should we seek out your father tomorrow?"

She paused, watching the wine swirl in the glass. "I think that we should wait and do some looking around first, find out how things are here."

"What do you mean?"

She stared down at the table, tracing the grain of the wood with her fingernail.

"Would Dolomon be looking for me if my family was still alive?"

He hesitated. "Why wouldn't he?"

"The only way that I could claim my father's kingdom would be if all legitimate heirs were dead. How do we know that he hasn't already killed them?"

Justin stared out the window for a moment before answering. "We don't know, I suppose. But if he hasn't, perhaps there is a chance for us to save them."

She nodded, taking a long swallow of wine.

"I'll talk to a few people tomorrow; we should find out fairly quickly what the status of your family is."

She nodded again, raising the glass to her lips. The warm feeling in her stomach was a comfort. She was surprised when he reached across the table and took her other hand.

"No matter what happens, you'll be all right."

She squeezed his fingers in response, only letting go when the serving woman brought their dinner a moment later. The meal passed with lighter conversation and it wasn't long before she was following him to the room. The furnishings were comfortable, and she was out when her head hit the pillow.

The next morning, she woke alone. This time, however, Justin had left her a note. He was off to learn what he could about the political climate. It was safer than if she were start asking questions; she may have left ten years ago, but people did have long memories. Someone might recognize her.

She cleaned up and dressed, examining her neck in the mirror. The slash wasn't gone, but the salve he'd been putting on every time they checked it had made it heal faster than she'd expected. The skin had already knit evenly together, and she decided to leave the bandage off of it.

Justin had left her a leather scabbard for the dagger, and she was pleased to find that it vanished into the folds of her skirt when worn low. She smiled. The dagger would be as hidden as well as it would have been in her bodice, but it would be much easier to access. The gesture was reminiscent of something that Bryan would do, she thought absently, tightening the belt.

Dropping the room key into her belt pouch, she retrieved her staff and set about exploring Bayside. Much of it was as she remembered, but the less-wealthy areas somehow looked poorer while the rich looked more ornate. She frowned. Her father may have used his family for political gain, but he had never let his people suffer for it. She walked the streets for most of the day and reached the castle in the late afternoon, shocked to find the drab green and black of Dolomon's family flying from the highest turret. Soldiers like those they had fought in the woods exercised on the front lawn in a show of strength.

Sandra scowled, rage threatening to boil over as she turned from the gate, not wishing to be recognized. Dolomon's control of the city would make finding her father harder than she'd thought it would be. She searched her memory, seeking the names of any allies who may be sheltering him or could tell her where he was.

The answer came in the form of a flyer posted near a weapons shop not far from the castle. The bold printing announced the public execution of the king and queen, scheduled for sunset that afternoon in the city square. She'd seen her father's crest and colors displayed discreetly nearly everywhere that she'd gone today; Dolomon must have been hoping to kill them all at once and make his dominance over her people unquestionable. Sandra's heart jumped into her throat as she looked to the west; the burning ball had begun to descend toward the horizon, and she was nowhere near the square. Taking off at a full run, she let her memory guide her through the maze of streets that made up the center of Bayside.

She was forced to a halt when she encountered a wall of people surrounding the dais at the center of the city square. Pushing her way through, she reached the front in time to see one of Dolomon's soldiers kick a stool out from under her mother's feet. She was shocked to silence along with the rest of the crowd as her mother twitched several times before the rope she hung by snapped her neck and she fell limp. Tears spilled down Sandra's cheeks as her mother's lifeless body swung slowly to and fro, open eyes staring into space.

Her father had watched the execution calmly, but even across the distance between them Sandra could see the horrific pain that filled his eyes. She wondered where her aunts and uncles were, further chilled by the thought that Dolomon had already killed them. A soldier was about to remove the stool upon which he stood when Sandra pushed through the last row of people separating her from the open space before the stage.

"Stop!" she screamed, drawing all attention from the dais. The man she remembered from her tavern and from the woods stepped forward and spoke, voice booming across the square.

"Princess Cassandra, welcome home. I must say that I didn't expect you to arrive in time for your own execution."

Guards surged forward and surrounded her, brandishing swords and daggers.

She locked eyes with him and gave him a slow smile, one that promised his death. Her returned it with a superior smirk and gestured for the guards to take her. The crowd leaped backward to avoid being caught in the fray. She smothered the grief threatening to overwhelm her. I won't fail my father like I did Maeve.

"Time to dance," she whispered softly. Justin may not be at her back but she could sense that he was close. He would let her fight this battle alone, only stepping in if she needed him.

Whispering a prayer to the sky for guidance, Sandra lost herself to the spinning staff and the movements of the men surrounding her. Somehow it was easier this time than it had been in the woods, as if the weapon was an extension of her hands and controlled by her thoughts. All that approached were sent limping back with shattered bones and bloody faces. Unlike the night in the clearing, none of their weapons reached her.

"Hold!" the dark-haired man called; the soldiers stilled and scurried away, forming a loose circle around her. She spun to a halt, twirling the weapon once over her head before bringing it to a stop in her right hand at an angle with the ground. He sauntered down the stairs and moved toward her, stopping just out of her weapon's reach. He'd seemed older when she'd last had a solid look at him, but now, mere feet away, she placed his age somewhere close to hers.

"You are skilled," he observed with a predatory smile.

"Are you Lord Dolomon?" she asked coldly, sizing him up.

"I am Jared, his senior lieutenant," the man replied, casually resting a hand on the hilt of his blade.

Sandra frowned. "I have no use for you. Where is Dolomon?"

His grin slipped. "Lord Dolomon is not here."

She laughed. "So he is too much of a coward to oversee the execution of those who rightfully rule here."

Jared scowled at her and drew his sword. "You dare call Lord Dolomon a coward."

Sandra laughed again. "I do. Were he a man, he would face me himself."

She fought not to step back as the rage in his azure eyes coalesced into a battering ram that pounded against her confidence. Her grip on the staff tightened as he struggled for control of his temper, lips finally curling upwards into a sinister smile. "How's your neck?" he asked silkily before springing toward her.

She slipped into the rhythm of the fight, focusing all of her concentration on parrying his attacks; he was the best that she'd ever faced. Blood trickled down her arms and between her breasts from where his blade kissed her skin, but she did not strike out herself, hoping to find a weakness. He danced back and they circled one another warily .

"Not so easy to kill, am I?" she taunted, spinning the staff slowly and ignoring the steady throb in her neck.

"I've not been trying all that hard," he said, lunging at her. She leaped back and twisted, sword passing a hairsbreadth from her throat. As he went by, he seized her arm with his free hand and dragged her against him, sword arm wrapped around her chest and holding her arms against her body. The surrounding crowd gasped, and she could hear angry whispers and scuffling as someone tried to push through.

"It didn't need to be this way," he whispered against her ear.

"How else would it be?" She snarled, stomping on his instep and trying to dart away as he growled in pain and his grip loosened. He managed to keep hold of her wrist and pulled her back, trapping her hands between their bodies and lowering his head to hers.

"I'd always wanted a wife with spirit," he murmured, words sliding over her like a caress.

Shock nearly overtook the anger coursing through her, and she realized that was exactly what he'd wanted. She brought a knee up, and he pushed her away as it connected. She stumbled back, regaining her footing as he straightened, smiling appreciatively through the pain.

"It isn't too late," he purred, silky arrogance returning as he approached. "We could rule together."

Fury overwhelmed reason and she sprang forward in attack, forcing him into retreat. Shock materialized in his eyes as she sent his blade flying across the green just before she closed them forever.

"I don't think so," she whispered, unable turn away from the still form. A wordless bellow drew her attention back to the dais where a man stood glowering at her.

"You killed my son," he roared, face twisted in hate.

He had Jared's dark hair except that it was streaked with gray, and his eyes were a copy of the man dying on the ground at her feet. There was no doubt in her mind that this was Lord Dolomon.

"You killed my mother, my friends, and goddess knows how many other members of my family," she screamed back, face contorted with sorrow that managed to slip through the wall she'd built around it. "Killing your son is nowhere near what you deserve." Dolomon's face reddened as strode across to where her father was watching her, seemingly fascinated.

"Yes, I did. Now I shall dispose of your father, and no one will stand in the way of my official acquisition of your kingdom." He kicked the stool out from under her father's feet and the imprisoned king hung free, struggling against the rope. She tried to run to the dais, but Dolomon's soldiers moved into a tight line, blocking her path with their weapons and triumphantly mocking faces. Sandra's father's eyes locked with hers, pleading for her forgiveness before his neck broke and his life was extinguished. She fought the urge to scream out, choosing instead to plant her staff in the ground and taunt his murderer.

"No one except me. And until I'm dead, you'll gain nothing."

He growled in anger and flew down the stairs, retrieving Jared's sword before he attacked.

Dolomon was not as talented with the blade as his son, but much of her strength had been drained in her duel with Jared. It took every shred of her focus to counter his father as they moved across the green, attacking and parrying in a complicated dance of near-misses and precise strikes. He'd drawn her blood with a few of his attacks, but favored his sword arm and his knee where she'd struck him with enough force to crack the bone. She fought the exhaustion and burning pain in her neck that threatened to shatter her concentration.

"I will have your father's kingdom," he barked, coming at her again.

"Not today," she shot back, blocking several quick strikes and hitting his wrist on her upswing, knocking the weapon out of his hand. He faltered, stunned when the blade flew through the air and landed with a clatter on the dais. She spun the staff with one hand over her head and struck his stomach and head in quick succession. He crumpled to the ground, fighting to draw breath.

Despite her fatigue she channeled her remaining energy into a graceful spin, drawing the dagger as she turned and dropping to straddle his chest with the staff over her head and the blade at this throat. His eyes begged her for mercy, but she had none for him. She hesitated only a moment before driving it through his neck and into the ground. His body spasmed beneath her before falling still. She pulled the dagger free and wiped it clean on his shirt, staring into his sightless eyes. It was done. She'd avenged Maeve and Dorian's deaths, and those of her family, but something inside of her still felt hollow.

The people gathered around them let out a collective gasp of shock, on the heels of which came an explosive cacophony of whispers, shouts, and cheers. She could feel their stares burning into her back. Dolomon's soldiers scattered, stunned by the sudden decimation of their leadership. The bodies of her parents had been taken down by soldiers that wore her father's colors and lay on the dais covered by white sheets as the men prepared stretchers to return them to the castle.

She rose and stepped back from Dolomon's body, sheathing the dagger and watching as his blood seeped into the ground. As the adrenaline drained from her veins, what she'd witnessed and what she'd done started to sink in. Involuntary tears welled in her eyes, and she forced them away. Dolomon and Jared deserved to die. It was justice. But somehow she still felt guilt for their deaths bubbling up through the crushing grief that had broken free and threatened to engulf her.

She jumped and spun around when a hand fell on her shoulder, pulling the blade once again. Justin leaped back, hands out in front of him in a gesture of submission. The crowed behind him quieted and abruptly and stepped away, white-knuckled hands clutching skirts and children's collars.

"Sorry," she murmured, putting away the weapon. A few of her father's soldiers appeared and started to clear the mob. No one touched the bodies of Dolomon and his son.

"Glad to see that it came in handy," he said casually, gesturing to the sheath that hung at her waist.

She stared at him, unsure of how to respond. The cavalier words were belied by a deep sympathy that radiated from his eyes. "They're dead," she said quietly. "I killed them."

"I know," he replied, moving closer to her. "I watched you do it."

She didn't answer, just stared at the ground.

"It doesn't feel any better, does it?" he asked softly, pushing strands of loose hair back from her face, fingertips gently brushing her cheek.

She shook her head, not lifting her gaze from the grass. He pulled her into a gentle embrace before leading her from the green and back to the inn. The lingering crowd parted before them without any prodding from Justin. Some reached out to touch her, fingers brushing against her hair, her back or her arms.

The city passed in a blur of doorframes and window panes framing shocked faces; her feet moved of their own volition toward the sunset blazing in the sky ahead. She didn't resist when he guided her to the bed and told her to sit, downing the strong drink that he pushed into her hands without protest. After retrieving his saddlebag, he unlaced her bodice and skirt and bandaged the cuts visible above her chemise before cleaning the blood from her exposed skin and tucking her into the bed with instructions to sleep. She curled into a ball around the pillows and did what he told her to, not awakening until the next morning.

She was alone, but the warmth of the space beside her told her that he'd not risen long before. She had sat up and was rubbing sleep from her eyes as he entered carrying a tray of breakfast. "Your sister is here to see you," he said neutrally, sitting facing her and setting the food between them.

She frowned. "Which one?"

"Allesandra."

"Why?"

"Honestly? I have no idea. You'll need to ask her that."

She stared at the food. "I'm not hungry."

"I know. But you need to eat."

She glared at him, but there was no malice behind it. He handed her a slice of toast before rising to answer a knock at the door. It was Allesandra, not wanting to wait until Sandra had cleaned up before seeing her. Sandra didn't speak as her eldest sister ordered her entourage to wait outside before crossing the room to take the space that Justin had just vacated. He left the room, cutting off the protests from Allesandra's guards as he closed the door and locked it behind him.

Sandra nibbled the bread he'd handed her and eyed her sister warily. Allesandra barely looked old enough to be six years her senior; her light brown hair showed now signs of gray, and no wrinkles marred the flawless skin. "You look well, sister."

"As do you; it appears that having grand adventures with a common soldier has agreed with you." Sandra bristled, but chose not reply harshly. Her sister was speaking with her, civilly, after years of absence. Besides, the words were true even if they were less than tactful.

"How is Matthias?"

"You remember my husband's name?" Allesandra asked, surprised.

"Of course I do. I may have been young when you married, but I was not oblivious. He was a kind man."

Allesandra smiled. "He still is, despite my inability this far to provide him with an heir. Many other men would have taken a second wife by now, but he continues to try."

Sandra shifted slightly, looking down at the quilt covering her legs. She and Allesandra had never been close; hearing about her sister's familial challenges made her uncomfortable after so much time apart.

When the awkward silence had stretched as long as she could bear, she took a deep breath and asked the question that had been at the front of her mind since Allesandra walked through the door.

"Not that it isn't lovely to see you, but what brings you here?"

"I want you to rule," her sister replied without preamble.

"Why?"

"Because it is your duty."

"Why don't you?"

"Because I already have a kingdom to oversee. You may be familiar with it; you've run a tavern there for the past five years.

Sandra was shocked. She hadn't realized that Allesandra ruled where she'd lived before. "Why did you never seek me out?"

Allesandra looked at her for a long moment before answering. "I think that I understood and respected your decision more completely than any other member of our family. I love my husband and have accepted my life, but a piece of me is jealous of you for taking control of your own destiny while I was used to gain father an alliance with Matthias's family. I presumed that if you wanted to see me, you would have done so."

"I didn't realize that you had taken on leadership of that area of the plains; our town council never announced it."

"I am not surprised. We made no changes in the taxes or laws. It was a peaceful acquisition—the former rulers were allies without heirs who approached us, wishing for a peaceful future for their people rather than the near-tyranny of the neighbors to the east."

"So you control the entire plains area, from the southern coast to the northern mountains."

"Yes," Allesandra answered. "And Lessia was married to Nathaniel Breen several years after you left. His family controls the northern mountain lands, reign stretching to the sea. If you assume control of the western coast, our family will have a hand in the rule of two thirds of the continent, at least for a little while."

Sandra nodded, brushing crumbs from her fingers. "Who is Dolomon and why did he come after us?" Jared's words to her during their duel had given her an inkling, but he could have been lying.

Allesandra hesitated.

"Please tell me," Sandra prompted, retrieving an apple from the tray.

"He was a local lord in the southern half of the kingdom with lofty ambitions. He wanted his son to marry you so that his family would play a part in ruling the coast. When you left, he took it as a personal affront and decided that he would become king, one way or the other. He managed to raise just enough support to secede that area from Alexandria and has been trying to take the rest since, but he barely has the manpower to maintain the lands he controls, to say nothing of conquering more."

"And he knew that. So since he couldn't oust father by force—"

"He tried to do it in a more clandestine way, occupying Bayside for a short time with just enough soldiers to keep the populace from rioting and the castle secure until he could murder the current monarchy and any relatives that could step into the void. He was betting that Father had sent most of the army out to guard the borders despite our advantage in strength."

"Which he had."

"Yes."

Sandra paused, twisting the blanket in her fingers. "Our aunts and uncles?"

"Dead. He sent his son after them, as he did you."

"How did you and Lessia escape him?"

Allesandra smiled. "Matthias and Nathaniel are rather…protective. Any soldiers suspected to be Dolomon's were killed on sight. He stopped sending them after three or four tries and simply threatened to kill us if we ever returned to Alexandria." She paused as if carefully choosing her words. "It is time to make our homeland whole again. His heirs will not be able to hold the south for long with their current numbers. The Alexandrian army will need to grow a bit to ensure an easy victory, but the kingdom needs someone with good instincts and strong convictions to lead it."

Sandra didn't answer.

"Please," her sister pleaded. "There is no one else."

Sandra stared at her, surprised. The thought of ruling in her father's stead was both terrifying and fascinating. She'd been struggling with the issue since coming to the realization that her parents may be dead, but she'd been expecting resistance from her surviving siblings, not to have them beg for her return.

"You've already earned the respect of his advisors and of the people of Bayside. That is more than you need."

She stared into her sister's green eyes, so like her own, and nodded. Allesandra was right—it was her duty. Perhaps taking on the rule of Alexandria was the new adventure that she was searching for. It would certainly not be boring, at least at the beginning.

The other woman let out a sigh of relief. "I'll speak to the council."

Sandra nodded again, staring at the tray that lay between them.

"So….this Justin that has been so protective of you. Is he your husband?"

Sandra laughed softly. "No, he isn't my husband." Allesandra looked disappointed.

"Perhaps you should consider him."

She nearly spit out the fruit that she'd just taken a bite of. "Why?"

This time it was Allesandra who laughed. "You must be blind to not see how he looks at you, my dear." Sandra opened her mouth to protest, but Allesandra continued before she could. "I will speak with the council this afternoon. They will want to meet with you soon. Shall I tell them that they can find you here?"

Sandra nodded, still preoccupied with what her sister had said about Justin. Allesandra leaned forward and kissed her forehead gently. "Welcome home, sister."

She smiled and grasped her sister's hand. Allesandra returned the smile and rose, leaving the room.

Sandra stared at the closed door until it opened again, and immediately looked down at the quilt when Justin stepped through. He sat across from her and took the last slice of toast from the plate.

"So?" he questioned.

"So what?" she replied nervously, twisting the blanket between her fingers.

He sighed in exasperation and picked up the tray, setting it on a table near the bed before returning.

"So what are you going to do? Fade back into obscurity, or take control of your homeland?"

She didn't bother to ask him how he'd known what Allesandra had been there to talk to her about. "What do you think I should do?" she asked, not meeting his gaze.

"It doesn't matter what I think," he replied, shifting closer to her on the bed. "What matters is what this tells you," he finished, reaching out and placing a hand over her heart. She stared at him and covered his hand with hers.

"I've decided to rule here," she said quietly.

His face broke into a smile. "Good."

She was surprised at his reaction. "Why?"

"You are a princess. It is your duty," he said in an echo of her sister's words. An awkward silence fell between them, his hand on her chest and her fingers tracing patterns on his skin.

"So what will you do now?" She asked, almost afraid of the answer.

He hesitated, watching her with that intense, unreadable look that she'd seen more than a few times over the course of their journey.

"Go back to the path I was on before I met you, I suppose," he replied, but something about the words felt forced to her.

"Is that what you want?" she asked softly.

He paused again. "Do you have another suggestion?"

She regarded him cautiously. If he rejected her, than he rejected her. At least she'd know. "Actually, I do," she said, reaching out and caressing his cheek with her free hand. His breath caught as she touched him. His eyes looked bluer than she'd ever seen them, like the ocean that had ruled her past and would shape her future. She realized in that moment that she didn't want to live her life without him, regardless of the choice that she made.

"Do you?" he asked hoarsely, reaching up to stroke the hand that lay against his face. Her skin tingled at his touch, as it had so many other times that she'd dismissed during the journey. She wasn't going to ignore it any longer.

"Yes," she whispered before leaning forward and brushing her lips against his. He trembled beneath her hand before cradling her face and deepening the kiss, exploring her mouth with a passion that was well hidden beneath his calm, collected exterior. Fire raced through her veins when he wrapped an arm around her waist and pulled her closer, mouth caressing her neck. She winced as his embrace sent shards of pain slicing through her, but she didn't cry out, not wanting him to let go. He raised his lips from her throat, brushing tendrils of hair from her temples and slipping his fingers into the mass of loose strands, gently drawing her eyes back to his.

"Are you sure that this…that I am what you want?"

"I've never been more sure of anything else."

There were no more words as he kissed her again, pushing her back into the softness of the mattress and stretching out against her. She didn't know exactly what the future held, but she did know in her soul that they would face it together.

NOBODY COMES HOME

~*~

Tamela J. Ritter

Author's Notes: This story was inspired by Cowboy, who wanted exactly the kind of story I wanted to tell. An American Love story.

~*~

The half-empty glass of water perspired, leaving rings on the chipped, decade-old stained counters of the diner. The sweat on John's upper lip had mixed with the condensation with each swallow, leaving a greasy film on the top of the glass, like the rainbow oil slicks on the scorched paved highway out the fingerprint-spotted window.

The bite-size ice chips that had once danced in sparkling reflected light with every forward tilt had finally floated away in the sunset, leaving various miniscule food particles in their wake.

John tried not to notice as he wiped at his forehead with the pink side of his bronzed arm once again. The beads of sweat deposited there were absorbed into his skin instantly. The day before had reached 102 degrees before the thermostat outside the diner's door had busted from exhaustion. This section of southern Wyoming wasn't prepared for these sorts of only-in-hell heat. The dusty fan going a top speed of five m.p.h. just wasn't creating any comfort for John and the lone customer hungry enough to clothe himself and go outside where no trees could shade and no car's air conditioner could fight.

Standing up from the stool at the counter where he was sitting, John hitched up his sagging pants back to the top of his hip. He could have sworn that the jeans had fit only that morning.

He took a hold of the empty water pitcher and slid open the ice machine's door. Sighing, he put his head farther in to smell the flavor of chill, to feel the sweaty hairs on his neck tingle from frost. Taking his time with the ice and popping one in his mouth as he went to the water, he studied his customer. He had resented the intrusion when he first saw the car approach the abandoned lot. John hadn't needed to rise from his seat at the counter for almost two hours and he was just beginning to wonder if anyone would notice if he went and took a nap in the walk-in cooler.

The customer had endeared himself to John almost instantly however, when he took a seat in one of the booths. (Counter seaters were chatters, and if one more person asked him "Hot enough for ya?" John was going to stab them with a rusty fork. *What kind of question was that anyway?)* He liked him more when he had only ordered two slices of apple pie ala mode and a glass of milk.

Looking to be at least in his mid-forties, the man had a lean figure with sunken green eyes and red short hair and scraggly beard covering a jutting chin. He was wearing a white t-shirt and faded jeans and looked oddly devoid of any signs of sweat. There wasn't even much of a glisten of moisture on the bald part of his head that the comb over didn't touch.

John took the pitcher and filled the customer's empty water glass. "Thanks Chief," the customer said.

John nodded and walked away. He had grown used to that nickname. Back when he first got a job off the reservation and people called him "Chief" he had bristled. It was an insult to his grandfather and to all his ancestors who were actual chiefs to be called that, especially since he was still in his twenties and hadn't even begun to earn that sort of title.

"Hey, how long it been this hot?" the customer asked.

John groaned inwardly. *Please, not the weather.* "This is the fourth day it's been over a hundred, nineteenth day since it's rained."

"Damn, that's gotta be some kinda record, huh?"

John shrugged, "Some kind."

"Say, you haven't seen a kid on a motorcycle stop in here today have ya?"

"No sir, you're my first customer since breakfast," John answered.

"Huh, he must be running late."

"What was that?" John asked against his better judgment. He was just about to return behind the counter and the peaceful barrier it offered.

"My son. We're supposed to be meeting here. He's coming up from Arizona and I came from Alberta. I can't imagine what's keepin' him."

John shrugged. "Maybe the heat. Ridin' open in these temperatures can't be pleasant. Why this place? Why meet here?"

This time it was the customer's turn to shrug, "It was halfway. I used to come in here when I was driving truck with my father back in the '60s and even back then it got no business and still stayed open. So I figured that even if the rest of the town had closed down, this joint would still be here."

John smiled. "There used to be a town here?"

The man laughed. "Yeah, hard to believe, but this used to be a pretty jumpin' 'burb. Close enough to Cheyenne to get the cowboys and cattle rustlers, and close enough to tourists spots to get them as well."

"Yeah, that's what they say. We still get the cowboys on their way up to the Montana ranches and rodeos, but that's pretty seasonal. The tourists though?

86

They don't wanna see Americana anymore. They want to see bears, or they wanna see celebrities at Sun Valley or Colorado, but not the people in between. People don't want to see normal people on their vacations. So they go places where they're surrounded by people just like them. People from the places they're from."

John walked back to his seat next to the dusty cash register, filled his own glass with icy water and looked down at the napkin he had been doodling on for way too long. He couldn't recognize anything he had written anymore. The thought of continuing on fruitlessly was even more depressing than amusing himself with conversation with a nameless stranger. "So, how long's it been since you've been back this way?" John asked.

The man was finishing his last bite of pie, dribbling cinnamon sugary apple onto his stubbly chin. After swallowing and wiping at his face with the much-used napkin, he answered, "Since before the war."

"'Nam?" John asked.

The customer's lip curled for a second. "Nam? You served son?"

"No sir," John answered realizing his mistake.

"Then you haven't earned the right to call it 'Nam, okay Chief?" The customer spat.

"Yes sir," John mumbled like a child who'd been reprimanded in the middle of a family reunion. Then, like most children in this situation would, he got resentful, turning away and, mumbling even lower, he said, "I haven't earned being called Chief either, but that don't seem to bother you."

Either not hearing him or choosing to ignore the comment, the customer threw his napkin on his plate. "Sorry, I should have never come back here."

"Here Wyoming?"

"No, here America. I've been living peacefully in Canada for the past six years. I should have never come back. This whole country puts me on edge. Sorry I snapped at you."

"No, I shouldn't have disrespected. I just have an uncle who served and he's always tellin' stories about his time over there and it's always 'Nam this and 'Nam that."

There was a long awkward silence that was only broken when the door creaked open and another customer came in. This customer caused John to smile widely.

"Cowboy, 'bout time cuz," John called out.

Cowboy, who looked anything but, with his long dark braids falling down to his chest and his dark skin showing through the tank top he wore with his faded Levi's, came to John, taking his fisted hand and pulling him into a one-shoulder man hug.

The new man smiled as he shuffled his feet. "Hey, sorry cuz, ya know, traffic was a bitch!"

They looked out the window as the dust settled back around Cowboy's piece of shit '69 Chevy truck and laughed. "Yeah, traffic. Could it be that you just woke up, ya lazy slob?"

"Shit man, what I gotta be up for? It's your fault I didn't get no sleep last night." He looked up and the sheepishness was replaced with a laughing tease as he whined, "Oh *Cowboy*, what am I gonna do without her? Oh *Cowboy*, hold me..."

"Fuck off," John said, trying not to smile at him, then he remembered the customer and it was now his turn to look ashamed, "Sorry sir," he mumbled as he walked back behind the counter. "What do you want?" he asked Cowboy, who plopped himself onto the furthest stool from the lone customer.

"Coffee. Just coffee."

"How can you drink hot coffee on a day like this?" John asked.

"Well, I'll tell ya what I've read. It is a scientific fact that hot beverages are the best things on days such as this; something to do with the molecular structure of the heated beverage and the break down of cooler drinks on the body's system. Besides, I think you have something hidden back there that will help cool me off." He said this last bit in a whisper and looked imploringly at his friend.

"Are you high? I can't give you anything. We don't have a liquor license."

"Oh come on cuz, I'm not asking you to *sell* me a drink. I'm asking you to sell me a coffee and then out of the kindness of your heart, to *give* me a little nip from your private stocks. For me, your truest most loyalist of friend who would—"

"Jesus, when did you become such a pain in my ass?" John said, reaching down beneath the register and taking out a small bottle of Irish whiskey.

Winking and toasting John with his newly-spiked coffee, he answered, "Last night. Don't you remember?"

"It is way too hot to put up with your shit. What are your plans for today?"

"Forget about my plans," Cowboy said in a lowered voice, looking over his shoulder into the corner where the customer was looking out of the window searchingly, "What's his story?"

John shrugged and told him what he knew; then cringed as he remembered that his best friend had absolutely no couth.

Cowboy turned towards the man. "Drivin' down from Canada, eh? Which province?"

"Alberta—Calgary Alberta."

"Ah Calgary. Had a few nights I barely remember up there." Cowboy chuckled. "Remember the Stampede of '80?" he asked, turning to John.

"Barely, but I do recall having to drag you away from a few girls you had mistaken for livery and were trying to ride all the way to the border."

Cowboy shooed this comment away and the customer visibly tried to hide his humor at the banter of strangers as he furtively eyed the parking lot.

"I'm sure he'll be here any minute. Would you like some more pie or milk?" John said.

"No thanks."

"How long it been since you saw your son?" Cowboy asked. John flashed him a look to tell him not to be so nosy, he ignored it.

"Last time..." the man stared out the window as if it were showing the movie of his life before he had wound up in this place with these strangers. "It was six years ago, last time I was here at all. When I got back from Vietnam."

There was silence while everyone did the math. Finally Cowboy began, "Okay, I'm not a genius by any stretch of the imagination, but the numbers aren't working right in my head. It's 1984 and you've been gone since 1978 and before that you were in Vietnam, but wasn't that war over in, like, '74?"

The man looked at them both and they looked down, Cowboy to his coffee wistfully and John at his cash register that seemed emptier then moments before. There was no reason to talk now; besides what would they say to this man? It become clear to John what this trip was about for him, what it meant to be in this diner, in this country waiting for a child who would never go through what his father had and will never know the sacrifice that made it so.

And almost as if wishing made it so, a bike came down the road in the southern horizon and there was a collective sigh of relief. Cowboy went back to the coffee, motioning to John to fill 'em up and he did so without the grief about the whiskey that he poured in as well. Taking a swig from the bottle himself, John watched the kid get off his motorcycle. After the guy took off his helmet, John was surprised to see the kid was probably only a few years younger then he was, making him about nineteen. John did the math again; this kid hadn't seen his father since he was thirteen years old. John shuddered.

The kid patted the dust off the baggy jeans covering his skinny, long legs and squinted back the way he had come. The white T-shirt he was wearing was stuck to his back with sweat and he rolled up his sleeves onto his shoulder as he meandered toward the diner, taking his time.

As the door opened, a small wind storm swirled around that caused him to cover his eyes and come in cursing. When he took his hand from his eyes and squinted around him, his first words summed up his attitude and feelings expertly. "What a shithole."

They all sat silently and watched him, waiting for him to more fully articulate his stance on the subject. "Seriously, how does anyone live around here? How have they not taken their own lives?"

Cowboy stood up and John laid a hand on his forearm. "Watch your mouth--" he began before John applied more pressure and Cowboy winced and sat back down.

The kid followed the noise to John and Cowboy who had taken their eyes off the offender and looked at the father for his reaction. There was a tangible uncomfortableness radiating from the customer who seemed unable to move from his seat as he watched his son scowl at their surroundings. The struggle to rise against the desire to hide under the table was evident on his face as he waited anxiously for his son to come to him. Finally, he stood up and the boy came over. They watched each other for a moment before the man put out his hand. The son studied it before he took it.

"Telly, how are you?" The man asked.

The boy shrugged and disconnected himself from his father's grasp. "I do okay, and you?"

Sitting back down, the man motioned the boy to do the same, John approached with a glass of water and a menu. Cowboy took the opportunity to reach over and refill his cup with John's behind-the-counter stash, never taking his eyes off the show on the other side of the diner.

"Anything good here?" the boy asked, and though John knew that is was a general question that gets asked a lot, almost a cliché really, he was still annoyed and defensive.

"No, not really."

The kid studied him. "Just a coke for now, thanks."

Walking slowly back to his place behind the counter, he heard the man ask, "So, how is your mother?"

The boy laughed mirthlessly. "I won the bet with myself. I knew that would be the first question you asked."

Blushing, the man tried to scowl. "Don't be a smart ass and just answer the question."

"What do you want to know? Does she miss you? Almost every day as far as I can tell. Has she moved on? Not really, although she has a few men trying to help her on that score."

"Don't be crude, not about your mother."

"Well, if you're so concerned, why don't you call her? You know she would love to hear from you."

The man said something quietly, so quietly that John and Cowboy had to lean toward them to make it out.

"I've hurt her enough. She thought I was dead for five years. Let her finish her mourning and get on with her life; I'm no good for her now. No good for anyone."

"She wanted to come with me," the boy said after a long silence.

"How did she know you were coming here to see me?" the man asked, alarmed.

The boy shrugged. "She found the letter. I'd never seen her so mad at me, and believe me; I've given her plenty of opportunities."

"I'm sure you have," Cowboy whispered to John, neither one of them bothering to pretend they weren't listening to every word spoken across the room.

The boy looked out the window and then turned in his seat. "Hey, what's there to do in this place?"

"This place?" John repeatedly dumbly.

"Nothing," Cowboy answered for him. "Nature and drinking, and sometimes drinking in Nature. I'm sure it's pretty much the same as where you live in Arizona, except no big gaping hole full of tourists."

"I live in Phoenix, which is nothing like this, thank God, and I've never even been to the Grand Canyon."

Silence and awe followed that statement. "Never?" John and the father asked at the same time.

"What's wrong with you boy?" Cowboy asked. "You practically live within walking distance to one of the seven wonders of the fuckin' world and you can't even bother yourself to go and even take a peep."

The boy looked ashamed for about a fraction of a second. "It's a fucking hole in the ground. Who cares?"

"You've never been there how would you know anything about it?" John asked, sounding deeply affected. "Forget about the tourists; forget about the other people altogether. You need to see it before you can say who cares. You can't call yourself a citizen of Arizona, forget about an American, if you haven't seen what is so great about it, let alone comment and dismiss it."

This time, the ashamed look lasted a bit longer and so did the silence from all that look meant.

"I never liked the great outdoors too much," the boy said, breaking the silence after a moment. Looking out the window and saying softly, "In Boy Scouts, it was always the father-son outings, and I never participated."

This comment was followed by an even longer silence that was broken this time by Cowboy. "You know what that calls for? What is absolutely necessary?" Everyone looked at him as he stood up almost bouncing. "A field trip. We have to show this boy the beauty of America all around him. Come on Johnny," he said turning to his friend, "show this guy what you are talking about, show him what he's missing."

"Are you insane Cowboy? These people don't wanna go on one of your crazy road trips," John said.

"Why not? What else are they gonna do? Check out the sites of downtown ShitHole, Wyoming? You think they drove all this way to have a slice of pie and then go their separate ways?"

"Okay, forget about them. *I* don't wanna go on one of your crazy road trips," John said in a slightly lower voice.

Looking highly affronted, Cowboy asked, "Why not? What else do *you* have to do?"

John looked around hands raised to show Cowboy around the diner. "Hello? Kinda working here."

"Oh shit, please. This place is a fuckin' tomb, cuz. I bet you cash money you haven't made more then a hundred dollars today, hell this whole weekend. What else you got stopping you? Your girlfriend? The one that left you for Seattle two weeks ago?"

John thought about it, trying really hard to come up with something, anything that would stop him from having to go and do anything. Looking over to the two in the booth, knowing they would answer for him, *they're not going to want to go on some crazy road trip with us Injuns!* he thought to himself. With horror, he watched them look at each other, think about it silently for a moment and then shrug.

Sighing, John said, "Okay, but I'm not driving all the way to fuckin' Arizona."

Now Cowboy did hop up and down, apparently amazed that something he suggested on a complete whim would actually happen. "No sweat. We both know a closer canyon, a better canyon. It still stands for America and everything that makes it worth fighting and dying for," at this he looked significantly at the man who had served and sacrificed and then left the country, "but that doesn't have quite the crowd surrounding it. Just as beautiful but not so overpoweringly grand that it causes you to question your own insignificance."

Cowboy and John looked at each other and, at the same time, said, "Bryce Canyon."

"*What* Canyon?" the boy asked.

John looked at him. "Bryce Canyon. It's in southern Utah and is quite possibly the best place in all the world, and although it's not as big as the Grand Canyon, it is much more beautiful and gives off the feeling that you might just be the only person who had ever discovered it."

It wasn't so much the words that John spoke but the particular shine in his eyes that convinced the other men that they must see this place and play their role in history. They looked at each other for confirmation, shrugged again and looked back to the Indian guides before them and nodded.

John sighed, went to the door and flipped the OPEN sign over, and turned back to them with a warning. "The first person to call me Sacagawea will find their asses on the side of the road in the smack dab middle of nowhere."

The man smiled for the first time in a while. "We won't call you Sacagawea if you don't call us Lewis and Clark."

John smiled back and took the man's hand as he got up and approached them. "Fair enough. My name's John; this is Cowboy."

They all shook hands and introduced themselves.

Half an hour later, they were on the 530 headed south, with a Willie Nelson cassette playing on John's Bronco and Cowboy sucking back the last bits of the Irish whiskey.

"So, why do they call you Cowboy?" the kid in the back seat called out over the sound of the twangy guitar and wind whipping in the opened windows.

"Why? I don't look like a Cowboy to you?"

"When we were growing up," John began, "Cowboy over here was a bit of a pansy ass runt and so when we went to play Cowboys and Indians, he was always stuck as the Cowboy. Got so he could take a scalping with the best of them. He's been Cowboy every since."

Cowboy beamed, as if proud of the name and its origins. "What does Telly stand for?"

His father answered for him. "When he was a boy his first complete sentence was, 'Daddy, telly me a story' and he said it all the time, 'telly me a story,' 'telly me a story.' And I would always say, 'okay Telly here's a story just for you.' It just sorta took and it's been Telly every since." It was the most the man had talked all day and the boy noticed it too.

"I don't remember that. I guess I never really thought about the origins. It was just my name, ya know?"

"I wish I had a cool nickname," John said, mostly to himself.

"Okay, how about...hmmm, oh I know; you can be Tonto. I'll be the Lone Ranger. You can even have a cool catchphrase like, 'look out Kimosabi'...what the hell does that even mean?" Cowboy wondered aloud.

"It means shut the fuck up or this red man will be pulling over and dumping your Kimosabi ass on the side of the Kimosabi road," John answered.

A moment later, when they had forgotten what they had been laughing about the man began softly, "Back in the day, I was called No Body."

"No Body?" his son asked.

John looked in the rear view mirror and saw the far-away look return to the man. He turned down Willie and listened to the private meanderings of his sorrowful passenger.

"Where we were kept." he began slowly, "It was very important that they know what our name and rank was. For some reason, it was very important for us not to tell them. Too important. So when it became apparent that they would win in the game, we gave our names. I was the first to break. On the nineteenth day without food, I was asked what my name was; I said 'No Body.' I was given a bowl of rice. Hendriks caught on and answered, 'Eat Shit' and Lawrence became 'All Day.' When they would come in the morning with our food rations they would say, 'No Body Eat Shit All Day.'" He smiled to himself at the memory. "It kept our spirits up for a long time after."

"I didn't know that either," Telly said. "Why didn't you ever tell me that story before?"

The man, still looking out the window, shrugged, "I couldn't talk about it for a long time. Besides, it really wasn't an appropriate bedtime story. Not for any son of mine."

"I would have liked to have heard it though."

Taking his role as uncomfortable silence killer very seriously, Cowboy inquired, "Who else is thirsty?"

They found a store off the highway and went in for some supplies. Coming back out, his pockets a lot skinnier after buying Cowboy's half rack of Schmidt's, two bags of Slim Jims and a dozen donuts for their rations, John looked to the sky and pointed something out to the rest of the party.

"What is it?" Telly asked.

"That is a Bald Eagle," John answered.

"Really?" the boy said, sounding excited.

"Yeah, they usually don't make it this far south."

"Look at the size of him," the man said in awe.

"Did you see any when you drove through Idaho? There are a lot of them there; they nest right on top of the telephone poles up and down the highway. It's really fascinating every mile or so to see an Eagle circling around its pole." John said.

"No, I missed them. I wasn't really spending too much time looking at the scenery. But I'll be sure to keep my eye out for them on the way back," the man said, almost as a promise.

Cowboy exited the store, ice bag over his shoulder and cigarette dangling from his lips. He looked up, said, "Cool," and proceeded to the truck. After filling the cooler, he took out four beers, handed one to John and the other two to the man, who looked at the beers, then at his son and then handed him one, swallowing hard.

The others, pretending that this wasn't a big moment—sharing your first beer with your father—got in the car and started back down the road. The car ride was quiet as they all chewed on their processed meat and other non-healthy junk foods that accompanied any road trip. John also blamed the silence on that each of them were probably ruminating about their first time they had sat with their father's and shared a beer.

John had been fourteen and not only had it been his first beer, but it had also been the first time his father had taken him hunting. The first kill and the first beer were simultaneous in all his recollections. The smell of blood as he had stood over the elk that he, to this day, didn't know if his gun or his father's had brought down, had always mixed with the smell of Budweiser in his mind. 'Only the best for this special occasion, son,' his father had said.

The many, many beers they had consumed in each other's company after that day had blurred into the story of their lives together. Until two years before when his father had died.

Cowboy's first beer had been with John's father too. Being raised by his mother, a slew of aunts and uncles, and a horde of cousins, he had liked John and his family more than his own and had adopted them as his pretty early on. They, in turn, had accepted him and his many foibles and flaws as theirs. So even though John's first hunting trip was just the two of them, father and son, the rest were not. They always had included Cowboy, bringing up the rear, or tromping excitedly in front of them, scaring all the prey away with his mindless chatter.

They made camp as the sun was setting into Fish Lake in the middle of Utah. While Cowboy went foraging for kindling and timber, John unpacked the Bronco of all the camping gear that he kept in the back, for just these occasions. As much as he had protested back at the diner, he really could never deny a chance to be out in the woods, could never deny Cowboy really. He just couldn't let him know that—ever.

That night they feasted on trout and wild mushrooms as John identified all the wilderness sounds around them. After some negotiations the father and son were talked into taking the tent and letting Cowboy and John sleep under the stars with the fire. It was probably the howls of the coyotes coming closer and closer that finally won the two men over.

After John and Cowboy heard the slumbering sounds from the tent they began to talk of other things. Living another man's troubles too long—while entertaining and distracting—couldn't erase things that were on your mind before they came.

"You know she wanted you to go with her?" Cowboy began, gazing into the fire.

"I know," John answered, staring at the rainbow of flames as well. If he had to think about it, he would have to say that most of their serious talks were directed at a fire of some sort. It was easier that way. "She understands though. I can't just up and leave. Not now."

"John, your momma will be fine. You think we'd all abandon her if you left? She would still have me."

John stirred the fire and bit his tongue from saying what was on its tip. *You can't even take care of yourself, Cowboy. You need my bailing you out and helping you just as much as she does, maybe more sometimes.* Instead, he said, "I know you'd be there and everyone else, but none of you know how she's been lately. Last week she showed up at the diner in full PowWow regalia begging for a ride to pick up papa in Cheyenne. She had a very detailed, realistic-sounding story to where he was and why he needed to be picked up, but she couldn't tell me how she had gotten the fifteen miles from our house to the diner.

"I know you think it was pride keeping me here. Like how dare she take a job in Seattle and expect me to follow her. But it's not that. She knew, knew about mama, knew what was expected of me, and she still left. She can't possibly expect me to follow her; maybe she never wanted me to."

"Maybe she wants you to come and bring her back. Maybe she needs a grand declaration of your devotion."

"Maybe you've been reading too many of your grandmother's damn Harlequin vagina books."

Cowboy laughed. "Maybe."

John stirred the fire, relieved that he had once more dodged the question of him having go and do anything.

Early the next morning, they chowed down on stale doughnuts and fireside coffee as they broke up the camp site in the hazy light of near dawn and hit the road again, heading southwest. John wanted to get them there at the exact right hour of the day. As he turned off the highway and traveled down the dirt road and the mountainous trees gave way to rich golden stone structures all around them, the sharp intakes of breath from his backseat passengers reassured him that he had chosen right. The tall pillars of fiery red and orange stone were beautiful in and of themselves, but when the sun was the right color of pinkish yellow, it was quiet literarily, breathtaking.

"Holy Jesus, what is this?" Telly asked. He had none of that cynical scorn from the day before so John couldn't be smug and point out that the boy had a lot of the same beautiful scenery within half a day's driving distance from his home.

"Those," he said pointing to the pillars, "are called Hoodoos."

About three miles down the road with mountains of rocks on their left and sagebrush on their right, they came to a place where John had to pull over. He'd never come to this place without having to get out and walk around it. Cowboy explained this to their passengers and they got out as well. It was a place where the manmade road met the natural world in a unique way. There was a stone arch that jutted across the road in an almost perfect arc, allowing cars to drive through the window it created. As a child, John had been saddened by this encroachment of man on nature, but his father had reassured him profusely that man had not made that hole, that it was a natural occurrence of water, wind, and rock. John had been skeptical at first, but then when he had gotten to the canyon and had seen what nature was capable of, given enough time and the right weather conditions, he believed and felt the need to stop and pay tribute each time.

He placed his flat palm against the wall of pinkish rust and instructed Telly to do the same, "Can you feel that?"

"Almost. What is it?"

"Welcome. It's the whole country welcoming you home. It's the wild west and the pilgrims; the working poor, businessmen, housewives, slavery's ancestors, elders, teeny bopper girls, the whole melting pot of America welcoming you home." He was talking to the boy, but looking at the father.

The boy turned to his father, "Can you feel it dad?" he asked.

The man timidly held his hand to the warm stone, "Almost," he murmured sadly, "Almost."

"Come on, this is nothing compared to what awaits us just down the road." Cowboy called from the passenger side of the truck.

The man was the last to take his hand away, as if trying one last time to feel the warmth of a long-sought after but never received Welcome Home. He finally shrugged and joined the others already in the car.

They got to the canyon right before the morning rush of tourists made their way with their campers, yappy dogs, and screaming children. John expertly led them to the optimal place to get only what they had come for and nothing they hadn't, namely other people.

As much as John wanted to jump out of the truck and show them all the sites and tell them about it all, he also wanted them to experience it like it should be the first time. Alone. Waiting until they were out of sight, John and Cowboy wordlessly got out of the truck together.

John headed to the trail that the other men had gone down. Cowboy, having already spent one night in lock-up previously for public urination, went back down the road to the restroom to relieve himself of the three beers he'd had since breakfast.

John thought they would be much further down the trail and had purposely slowed his pace to make it so. They had found his favorite spot where the rocks rose out of the canyon in uneven spikes with many alternating layers of rust, orange, and red. John's father had told him that the rings of the color in the canyon walls were similar to the rings of the tree trunk, but instead of each ring representing a year, each symbolized a millennium of time.

This father and son stood side by side and observed the vast space before the two of them. John imagined that they were just like he and his father doing the same thing. He could feel that they saw it the same way, as if the canyon were put there just for them. Although the canyon would be there centuries and centuries longer then the men, it had changed some unperceivable way from the men's presence. That's what John had thought each time he'd been there.

They all stood there and watched the sun play on the wall of rock and felt the wind start to blow a chill breeze, as opposed to the scorching heat it had been blowing the last week. John looked into the distant horizon and saw the dark clouds form and move slowly, very slowly towards them. He smiled, and as he did so the father turned and looked at him with glassy eyes, smiling too, and it was as if they were smiling for the same thing.

"I feel it now," the man said.

John nodded his head slowly as the son turned to his father and said, "Welcome Home, Dad."

Putting his arm around his son, they walked back up the trail. Waiting for them on the trail head was Cowboy who looked like he had done something he was either very proud of or extremely ashamed of.

"Come on, let's go. Days a wastin' and it's my turn to drive."

"Are you high?" John asked, fishing for his keys.

"You know the rule; you drive to, and I drive from. Besides, I know the best place for an enchilada and margarita lunch."

John threw him the keys. "Fine, as long as it's not in actual Mexico." Then as he got in the passenger side he said, "You know, I only made that agreement because you are usually passed out for the drive back and I never have to actually follow through."

Cowboy started the truck with a wild dance in his eyes. "Don't I know it? But not today my friend. I am lucid, I am vertical, and I am driving."

Thirty minutes later, as they passed over the Utah/Arizona border, John reconsidered his decision. "Jesus Cowboy, where are we going for this lunch?"

"Relax, we're almost there," Cowboy soothed, flashing John a look that made him groan. The look said, *what ever maniacal plan I have cooked up, you, my friend, are in on in, whether you want to be or not.*

However after another ten minutes when the car started to stutter and smoke began to rise from under the hood, John could care less about any plan. "Fuck Cowboy, pull over."

Cowboy did as he told and trying to soothe him said, "I'm sure it's nothing."

John flashed him a look of his own that needed no interpretation as they got out of the truck and popped the hood.

"What the hell? I just filled the radiator yesterday morning."

"I know. I emptied it today," Cowboy said.

"What?" John turned on him.

"Well not completely, just enough to get us in this predicament. Relax. Just go with me. I know what I am doing."

"Since when?" John scowled.

Cowboy looked at him with his basset hound eyes and John felt bad. "Sorry, so what is this all about?"

"Let's just call it our good deed for the day."

"I thought back there was our good deed."

"We'll let's just say the gods will owe us after this one. Now, I'm going to take the boy to the nearest town and you and pops are going to stay here as you pretend to know what you are doing under here."

"Hey, I know…oh alright, Mr. Mechanic. Go and get your help, but whatever you got cooked up better be done in the next couple of hours; those storm clouds don't look like they're going to be dumping candy sprinkles."

Cowboy smiled and went to the passenger side window. "Hey kid, ya wanna take a walk with me? There's a phone about a mile in a half up the road. We should be able to call someone to come and help us out."

This time, he gave The Look to the boy, who seemed to pick up on it much faster than John had. The kid practically smacked Cowboy in the head with the door in his rush to get out. "Be right back dad."

Before the father could say anything, they were specks along the deserted road.

If the man suspected anything, he didn't let on. "Do you think they'll be able to get anyone to come all this way?"

John shrugged. "I'm sure they'll persuade someone. Cowboy can be almost forcible persuasive when he wants to be."

The man smiled. "Yeah, I noticed that. He's a good kid though huh?"

John smiled too. "Yeah, actually he's the best, and even when he's not, he does it from a good place so you can't stay mad at him."

"I noticed that too. So, is there anything we can do while we wait?"

"You know anything about cars?" John asked, hoping the answer would be no.

"No, not really my specialty," the man answered, seemingly oblivious to John's sigh of relief.

"Me either, but I've been reassured by Cowboy that it should be no problem."

"So we'll just wait."

"Yep," John said, then after a minute he began, "Hey can I ask you something? If you don't want to answer you don't have to, but I've just been wondering."

"What?"

"How does a Vietnam P.O.W. war hero wind up returning and moving to Canada?"

The man looked out in the distance. "What makes you think that P.O.W. and war hero are synonymous? It is very possible for them to be almost contradictory."

John didn't need to express his confusion; the look he gave said it all. The man continued, "Sometimes the things a man does to survive are the very things that make him less than a hero."

Fighting the urge to ask him for more—instinctively knowing there is a limit to how much a complete stranger will tell another on the side of the road—he just nodded. But then he couldn't help himself. "Is that why you haven't seen your wife and son in all this time?"

The man shrugged, bent down and pulled up a dried weed, wiped it on his pants, inspected it, then deposited into his mouth. "You have a father right? How would you like one that woke every night in a cold sweat, screaming jibberish, whipping out his bowie knife that he can't sleep without? A father who can't look himself in the face without seeing all those things they were calling all of us on our return, knowing that they were true, but knowing something they will never know, the screaming never goes away, the faces of the dead—friend and foe—will never stop. How would you like a father like that, a spouse like that?"

Now it was John's turn to stare out into the distance and shrug. *Me and my stupid questions,* he thought to himself. But what he said was, "Every man has demons. I'm not comparing my father's self-imposed demons to what you experienced, but every son should have the right to decide for himself whether they want to be a part of their fathers' life.

"Having just recently experienced the loss of my father, all I can say is that I would take all the demons, the nightmares, the fights and misunderstandings and multiply them by a hundred if it would give me just one more day of having my father with me, and I know my mother feels the same way."

"It's too late for that now. I'm no good for a woman like her."

John looked horrified and couldn't help himself asking, "They got your pecker?"

The man laughed. "*Man* you are *young*. No they didn't get my pecker, it still works. But there are more important ways to disappoint a woman."

"Again…shouldn't she have a choice? Have your ever given her a chance to be disappointed?"

"What am I supposed to do? Drive to Phoenix, battle with all her other suitors, men with more money, more prospects, more—"

"We have no control over what a woman wants, what she needs. We can only be there when we can." Saying this, John thought of last night and what Cowboy was saying to him about his own female entanglements. *Damn Cowboy!*

The man watched him for a while, before looking away into the sky. It was an infinite passage of time before either of them spoke again and then it was the man who said, "Looks like rain."

John couldn't help laugh. *The fuckin' weather. I have reduced him to talking about the weather.*

"Yeah, 'bout time. I hope they hurry."

The thunder beat them, but only barely. They saw the men approach, munching on nacho chips and drinking out of large Styrofoam cups, as they watched the lightening fork in the sky.

"Cuz, good news."

"What?" John asked, eyeing him for a clue that his flimsy plans had worked themselves out. All he saw was large bags on food.

"They had To-Go Margaritas," he said with a cheesy grin, handing him a bag with two more Styrofoam cups.

"You're an ass," John said, taking his beverage out and handing the other to the other man. "So, did you get us any closer to getting out of here?"

"No, I went all that way for fuckin' Mexican. Yes, I took care of it, or actually *we* took care of it. Telly over there called someone to come and get him and his father and we have one of the locals coming to do his magic in that there radiator. He'll just have to finish his runs first. So in the meantime," he held up the other bags, "lunch."

They gobbled down what truly did turn out to be the best enchiladas that John had ever had, along with chips, guacamole, beans, rice and some fruity, doughy, fried something-or-other. Since the wind was cooling, but not wet yet, they sat on the side of the road and Cowboy tried to pass the time by telling humorous stories that seemed to get more and more convoluted as he began making slurping sounds on his Big-Gulp sized beverage.

It was right about the time that Cowboy started eying John's unfinished drink, and Telly snarfed rice and beans out of his nose at Cowboy's description and pantomime of his first and only attempt at bull riding that a brand new Honda Odyssey pulled up.

Telly, whose second time drinking with his father had a much more dramatic affect on him than his first, ruined the surprise of the new car's arrival by jumping up and running to the car, "Mommy, you're here!"

The blood left the man's face as he stood up to look. John and Cowboy exchanged glances.

"Mommy?" John whispered. "He calls her mommy?"

Cowboy blushed, "We had a lot of time to kill at the restaurant to give her some time to get here. The boy might have had a few too many margaritas."

The woman who got out of the truck was stunning, tall and thin with long legs and tight pants. It was like a fashion model just joined them, or at least a fashion model's older sister. Telly ran to her, and as she took him in her arms, she looked over his shoulder to the other man who stood up behind the Bronco.

Part of John and Cowboy wanted to skulk away and the other, stronger part, wanted to peek their heads over the hood and watch. They nudged each other and hunched up behind the hood. The man walked slowly to her, she walked slowly towards him, the boys on the other side of the hood almost ahhhed.

"Hey Penny," he said.

"Hey Odie," she said back, "You need a ride?"

He shuffled his feet like a schoolboy, "Yeah, that would be nice."

They walked back to her van, father and son both stopping before getting in, "Thank you John, Cowboy, truly for everything," the man said.

The boy, who looked truly like a little, happy boy waved too. "Yeah thanks for showing me America!"

They got in and drove away just as the rain began to pelt down in little plops.

John looked at Cowboy and Cowboy looked at John.

"You know what man?" John asked.

"What?" Cowboy asked waiting for a set-up to a joke.

"You're a good person. You know that?"

Cowboy blushed. "Ah, thanks man. 'Bout time you saw. Ready to go home?"

John thought about it and thought about the last day and then the last two weeks and it dawned on him, "No. I don't think so."

Cowboy stopped and looked at him. "Yeah?"

"Yeah, you were right. I won't know until I know. I'll probably be back in a week, but," he laughed with the fear of it, "maybe not."

"Okay man, let me get the coolant from the back and get this baby started again."

John followed him. "You knew this would all come together, didn't you?"

Cowboy shrugged. "You hope for the best."

"How do you think it will work out?"

"Ah who knows? They'll probably wind up killing each other. But as long as they do it together, right?"

"Right."

A NIGHT OF SURPRISES

~*~

N. Apythia Morges

Author's Notes: The inspiration from this story came from a mish mash of responses, mainly Drew's and The Gov's, but several others will see bits of their responses throughout.

~*~

"But I don't get it. I mean, if the crocodile swallowed a clock, wouldn't it have either killed it or he would have passed it? I mean it's not likely that you'd hear the clock ticking, especially years later. Crocks have thick skins and all. Not to mention that those teeth would have torn it to pieces."

"Yeah but how else would Captain Hook have been able to tell the difference between that crock and the others? He already lost a hand. Isn't that enough?"

"Are there even crocs in the ocean?"

"It was Neverland dude. Crocks could go anywhere."

I sighed and sat down at the table between Drew and Keith, whose political ambitions were obsessive to the point he asked us all to refer to him as The Governor. We had agreed to meet at Quiznos for a quick lunch and to go over everyone's last minute assignments for Kathy's surprise party.

"Hey, Gina, tell him there aren't crocs in the ocean," Gov said pointing a finger at Drew.

"It's fiction. The crocks could go wherever Barrie wanted them to go," I said with a shrug.

"I'd like to have a drink with Captain Hook. He was a man of great ambition," said Gov.

"He got eaten by a crocodile," I pointed out.

Gov drew breath to start an argument, but I cut him off. "Did you order the cake?"

He glared at me, obviously aware of my topic-changing tactics, before assuring me that the birthday cake would be ready for pickup after three tomorrow.

"Good. And did you hear back from the last of the guest list?" I asked Drew.

"Yeah, we'll have about fifty people there. I told everyone to bring some food."

I nodded. That should take care of snacks. As the party would be held at the bar, alcohol was not needed. The cake was ordered. That only left entertainment. "Did you book a band?"

"Naw," said Drew. "It would be too obvious if random musicians just showed up. Besides we got the juke box."

"Fine," I sighed, knowing it was too late to find someone to play now. "But no *Son of a Preacher Man*. I'll be picking up Kathy to go to dinner at five. I'll drop off all the decorations at Drew's beforehand. Think you two can handle getting the place ready?"

They looked affronted that I even asked. I replied with a pointed stare of my own, remembering the Christmas decoration fiasco. They looked away first, grumbling their assurances. I smiled. "Now that that is settled, I am off to go dress shopping. Call me if you have any problems." I placed a friendly kiss on each of their cheeks and ran my hand through Dew's Fabio-like hair before leaving them to their sandwiches and Captain Hook discussion.

I made another lap around the store, willing for that perfect dress to just jump out at me. Mitch was coming into town tonight and would be at the party. I hadn't seen him in weeks; he was always traveling someplace or another with work. The last time we met up at the bar, there was a certain something between us. Of course, it could have just been the vodka, but the romantic in me refused to believe that.

I wanted to look good. Yes, it was Kathy's party but that didn't mean I needed to look like an extra from *Freaks and Geeks*. It was nearly four. This was the third store I had been in, and I was determined not to go home empty-handed. I ruled out black right away, too cliché. Red just screamed "I'm easy." Hell would freeze over before I wore anything pastel.

I had just about completed my last lap when I saw it. There, smooshed in the clearance rack, was a swatch of chocolate-colored perfection. Grabbing it, I made a run for the fitting room. The simple sleeveless, V-neck sheath gently skimmed over my body, hugging my curves without being obvious. The color brought out my tan and complimented the golden highlights summer had bleached in my normally mousy brown curls. Perfect! And it was seventy-five percent off. Score! *Add a new pair of strappy heels, and Mitch won't be able to resist*, I assured myself as I handed the cashier my credit card.

Looking in the rearview mirror, I adjusted a hairpin to make sure an errant curl stayed in place before touching up my lipstick.

"What's up with you?" Kathy asked as I threw my lipstick back in my purse. "I've never seen you primp so much just to hang out here."

"Mitch may stop by tonight," I said with a silly smile.

Kathy laughed. "That explains the dress. I didn't think you got all fancied up just for me."

"What's wrong with two ladies getting all pretty for an evening out?" I asked, exiting the car.

"Nothing at all," Kathy grinned. "Especially if you want to be the Pretty Pretty Princess. But I know you better than that."

"True." I said following her to the bar. "But if anyone is going to be a Pretty Pretty Princess tonight, it will be you, Birthday Girl."

With that, Kathy opened the door to her bar to a chorus of "Surprise!"

"I'll get you," she mouthed to me before being whisked away in the crowd of well-wishers.

I scanned the room to find Drew and Gov huddled in the corner. As I walked over, Drew poured himself a generous double shot of bourbon. Gov's rum and Coke looked more than a little light on the latter. "Well done guys," I said pulling up a bar stool. "The place looks great."

"It's all thanks to my staple gun," Drew said proudly.

"What?"

"Well the tape wasn't holding to well," Gov started.

I raised my hand, cutting him off. "Never mind, I don't want to know. When Kathy asks, I'll be sure to give you two full credit for the decorations."

They raised their glass in a toast to me. It was then I noticed that maybe the point of sobriety for these two for the night had already passed. "Are you drunk already?"

"Noooooo," said Drew, drawing the word out into about ten syllables, shaking his head, is long hair flowing around him.

"With the staple gun, decorating only took about 15 minutes so we decided to start celebrating a little early," Gov explained.

"I see that," I said reaching over to take a sip from his glass.

"Get your own," he said prying his drink from my hand.

"Hey, watch the dress!" I stepped back to avoid alcohol being splashed on it.

"And why are you so prettied up?"

"No reason, I —"

"It's for Mitch, isn't it?" Drew said, smiling knowingly.

"And what if it is?"

He just shrugged. "The cake is in the kitchen," he informed me before standing. "I'm off to say hello to the birthday girl." He disappeared into the crowd, his hair whipping behind him.

My attention wandered to the other people in the room as I searched the crowd for the tall man with long, black hair.

"He'll be here," Gov said, drawing my attention back to him. "I had drinks with him in the city last week."

"Really?" I tried not to sound too interested.

"He asked about you."

"What did he say?"

"He wanted to know if you were a lesbian."

"A what?" I asked shocked. Then I saw the glint in Gov's eye. "You bastard!" I said playfully slapping his arm. He just grinned and took another swig.

"Go easy on that tonight," I warned him. "I'm not going to drag your drunk ass home."

"As if you'd ever take me home." He looked solemn. "You're nothing but a tease."

We were laughing so hard that I didn't hear someone approach behind me.

"Hey Gina."

Startled, I turned to find Mitch.

"Hey."

"I'm gonna go find Drew," Gov announced before taking his drink and joining the rest of the party.

"Nice dress," Mitch said, his eyes following the fabric to where it stopped a few inches above my knees. "Very nice."

I tried not to blush too much as I thanked him.

"It was great that you could make it," I said trying not to sound too stupid but I was having trouble coming up with intelligent conversation.

"I wouldn't miss Kathy's party for anything. You never know what kind of stories you will get out of events like this," he said with an almost predatory grin. His face faltered slightly when he looked closer at the H in the Happy Birthday sign. "Is that stapled to the wall?"

"Yeah, Drew and Gov decided to decorate with power tools."

Mitch laughed. "Were they already toasted?"

"Probably."

A silence fell between us, the kind where neither of you know what to say but no one wants to seem stupid and bring up some lame topic like the weather so no one speaks. It was Drew who saved us.

"Hey you two, stop being antisocial and come join the party."

Mitch offered his arm. "Shall we?"

I tucked my hand into his elbow and allowed him to lead me over to the couch.

"Having a good birthday party, Miss Pretty Pretty Princess?" I asked Kathy as I waited for Mike to pour her a shot of Citron before requesting another glass of Pinot Noir and a Sam Adams.

"Yes I am." She said each word as if it were its own sentence. "Thanks again for the journal; it's gorgeous. And thanks for organizing this."

"Anything for you babe," I said. "Besides, believe it or not, I did have some help from Drew and Gov."

"They were the ones to staple the decorations?"

"Do you need to ask?"

She laughed. "No. In fact, I am surprised either of them can still stand."

"They are rather drunk, aren't they?"

"They apparently are having a contest to see which should hold the title of Town Drunk."

"I see." I watched as the two stumbled about, matching looks of determination on their faces. I knew that could only mean trouble. I just hoped I wouldn't be caught up in whatever they had planned.

"Where did Mitch run off to? You two seemed pretty cozy chatting it up on the couch."

"He stepped out to make a phone call."

"Talking about me?" He asked, his mouth right next to my ear, causing me to start.

"How do you do that?" I asked, turning to face him.

"Do what?"

"Sneak up on people like that."

He shrugged. "It's magic."

Kathy shook her head with a laugh and walked away.

"So," I said.

"So," he whispered.

His eyes locked on mine and I could read the desire in them. My heart was pounding as my world was reduced to just his lips. His head slowly lowered toward my mouth. Just as his lips were about to close on mine, a startled scream caught my attention.

In slow motion, I turned my head to see the two drunks carrying the cake out of the kitchen. Gov tripped over a chair, and his end went flying out of his hands. Drew tried to save it, but a cake to serve fifty was too much for one inebriated man. The cake was airborne. I watched in horror as it descended. I tried to step out of the way, but there was no time.

Time snapped back to normal speed as whipped crème icing collided with my face, slid down my dress and landed with a splat on the floor. I looked up at Mitch whose own face was smeared with white frosting, and I didn't know whether to laugh or cry.

Mitch shoved me aside and lunged after Gov. I slid on cake, and my fancy heels went out from under me, leaving me sprawled on the floor, willing the ground to open up and swallow me whole. I wasn't sure if the flashes of lights were from the cameras or my head connecting with the floor. I was betting on the former if the laughter was any indication.

I opened my eyes to find Kathy's face hovering above mine as she brilliantly tried to fight her laughter. "Come on," she said, extending a hand, "You're flashing everyone."

"Great," I replied feeling my skin heat. "As if being covered in cake and falling on my ass wasn't bad enough."

As if to accentuate the point, Drew called out "Nice panties!" from across the room. He apparently had escaped the wrath of Mitch who was currently trying to suffocate Gov in a bowl of dip.

"This wasn't quite how I planned this night," I said, wiping icing off my face with a towel Kathy handed me.

"Honey, things never go the way we plan them," she said.

"Sorry about your party," I said.

"There's nothing to be sorry for," she said. "I haven't had this much fun on my birthday in years. It will be even better watching Gov mop the floor later."

"Hey," she yelled to Mitch who now had Gov in a headlock. "Let him go. I don't want to have to fill out paperwork if either of you get hurt." She stalked over to them to let them know she meant business.

Mitch released Gov and stormed out of the bar without so much as looking at me. I willed myself not to cry. Gov came over and put his arm around me, pulling me tight against him, coating me with sour cream and onion dip in the process.

"I'm sorry, Gina," he said sincerely.

I shrugged. "It was an accident."

"You have icing in your ear," he pointed out, trying to be helpful. I didn't care.

"My dress is ruined."

"Don't worry. Dry cleaners can work wonders. They'll make everything right as rain." He gave me a lopsided grin that told me he wasn't just talking about my dress.

"Thanks, Gov," I said giving him a hug, no longer caring about the dress or Mitch.

"Come on. Let me give you a ride home," he said.

"I told you I wasn't taking you home tonight."

"No, I am taking you home."

"You can't; you're drunk," I pointed out.

"Oh, yeah."

There was a long pause.

"Go on back to the party, Gov. I'm just going to go."

He flashed me one more smile before going back to join Drew as they serenaded Kathy with a rendition of Two Drunk Men and a Guitar.

I sighed, heading toward the kitchen to grab a roll of paper towels. I didn't want to have to clean cake off my car seat as well. Without a word, I slipped out of the bar, the breeze hardening the icing in my hair. *So much for being a Pretty Pretty Princess.*

LITTLE BLACK DRESS

~*~

Jill Bodach

Author's Notes: The inspiration from this story came from the Governor's bio – loosely. For some reason, it triggered the image of hopeless romantic who suffers great personal tragedy. The little black dress was probably meant to be a kinky addition to the story, but instead it became the central theme of this sad romantic tale. Yes, the author owns her own little black dress.

~*~

If you were to ask me what it was that did it to me, what turned me into what I am today, I'd tell you that I don't know exactly how it happened but I do know that it involved a dress.

It wasn't just any dress and the person wearing it wasn't just any woman but you probably figured that out by now, didn't you? Something so powerful that it can change your life had better be beyond extraordinary or else everyone will look at you and wonder how you succumbed to something so mediocre, why you don't have a better story to tell and why you don't at least lie to make it sound more impressive than it actually is.

My story is pretty impressive on its own and I'm not just saying that because it's mine. I've told it over and over again and each person I tell gets that look like they want to cry for my sorrows but know that I've probably cried enough tears, and theirs would seem miniscule in comparison, like filling a bathtub with an eye dropper.

Anyway, my downfall was a dress. A little black dress. Every woman has one, don't they? It's that one dress that makes them feel stunning, makes them feel like, yes, they do understand how the power of one woman could lead men to battle; makes men feel ready to draw their own sword if need be.

I was with her when she bought it.

She was holding tightly to my hand as she always did in that way that made me feel like I was special but when she saw the dress she let out a squeal and I knew that whatever the squeal was for, she'd have to have it and I'd have to do whatever I had to do to get it for her.

She asked if I'd mind if we went into the store. I never minded about anything she asked, and she didn't really ask for much. But even if she had, I would have given it to her. It's just the way things worked in those days. Now they don't work at all. Now someone asks me for something simple, like a Philip's screwdriver and I hardly remember which aisle to point them down, but I remember the floral design on the bottle of perfume that used to sit on my night table and the way the smell of it always told me she'd come home.

The dress was short with thin straps, spaghetti I think she'd called them. The hem of the dress fell just above her knee as she held the dress up to herself but it was the way it fell that she liked the most.

"It doesn't just lie there," she'd said, holding it out in front of her and then pulling it close again. "It's like a wave. See how it bounces? I guess you can't see it just by me holding it like that. Here, let me try it on. Will you wait? I want to hear what you think?"

I knew before she even put the dress on that I'd love it on her. And I had.

She was right, the hem did sort of dance above her knees while the rest of it clung tightly to other parts of her body. The back was wide open, looping down toward the small of her back and then coming back up like a bird that nose dives into the water to catch a fish and then rises suddenly with his prize. Tiny silver sequins decorated the thin straps and several gathered in a cluster at the dress's lowest point as if to remind the person looking that he was seeing something special. She sparkled in that dress.

"I never had a little black dress," she said. "I just...I never found one that felt right on me, you know? Not like this. What do you think?"

I could barely express to her what I thought, and it had little to do with the dress. I got down on one knee, right there in the dress shop, and asked her if she'd marry me. She thought I was kidding at first, just my way of telling her how great she looked. But I wasn't kidding, even though I didn't have the ring to make the proposal formal. She cried then when she realized it was the truth and then she pulled me to my feet and hugged me. I remember wanting to hug her tightly but being afraid I'd ruin her perfect dress. After we kissed and she cried, I paid for the dress. She wore it home.

Her little black dress.

I won't tell you where that dress is now. It would ruin the fun, or the misery, of my story. Either way, I'm not going to tell you where that perfect dress is right now. But I will keep telling you my story. And now that you know about the dress, you have to know about the woman. The dress worn by the most beautiful woman I'd ever seen. That's how life goes, isn't it? You have something wonderful and then, because you think it's too good to be true, you turn back to see it and it all turns to sand and all your left with are the pieces of something wonderful that doesn't at all resemble what it was before it fell apart.

There are some parts I am going to leave out and I hope you don't mind. I hope you'll understand that this is the only tale of any value that a guy like me will ever have to tell and if I give it all away, I'll have nothing left and I just can't do that. Don't worry. I'll tell you most of it. But the rest, that's just for me. Don't judge me or be angry with the way in which I share this with you. It's my story. I'll tell it how I want to. You can take from it whatever you want. That part is up to you.

I'll tell you that her name is Sara, although that doesn't tell you much about her at all. In fact, that name is ordinary and common and she was neither of those two things. Her name should have been Persephone or Anastasia. Something with more than two syllables that took you a long time to say. It somehow cheated her that her name was so short and took up so little attention by the speaker. I always wondered how her parents gave such a perfectly stunning child such a plain name. Couldn't they tell even when she was just a pink, squirmy, bug-like creature in a blanket that she would someday be something great, already was from the moment she took her first breath?

I can tell you that she had blond hair but again that doesn't mean very much. Blond hair is common, mainly because of that line that blondes have more fun and so a lot of women make themselves blond just to see if it was true. I certainly had more fun with her than I'd ever had before so maybe the saying is partly true.

Her hair cut was common too, cut just to her shoulder – never longer, never shorter. But I never lost her in a crowd. There was something different about her haircut, or maybe it was the shape of her shoulders, the way they curved under my hands. Either way, she took something common and made it uncommon. She did that a lot. I guess that's the point I'm getting at about her.

And I could tell you that her eyes were green, that she was 5'5, 5'7 if she was wearing heels, and that she had a birthmark right in the middle of her chest that she hated but I thought gave her character. I told her once that I thought the birthmark was there because her heart was so big that it was bursting out from inside of her but she had just frowned and said that was a gross thought and kissed me like she always did when she didn't want to make me feel too badly. I had kissed her back, unable to explain that all I'd meant by what I'd said was that I didn't understand how a heart so full of love and compassion could fit inside her small frame. How did her body contain all that love, that kindness, without it seeping out through her skin?

All those things would certainly give you a picture in your mind but it could give you the picture of any blond woman with the name of Sara who had a curious-looking birthmark. And what does that really tell you? It tells you nothing at all. Not when the woman we're speaking about is my Sara. So toss away whatever you think you know about her. Dismiss all your stereotypes and forget your preconceived notions. You don't know her, not even a little, and even if I wrote forever, which I just might do because what will I have when my story is told except those pieces I told you about that aren't ever going to be yours to share with me, you still wouldn't know her. And you wouldn't know me because I am not sure who I am without her. That sounds like the most depressing thing anyone has ever said, doesn't it? But it's true. And that's the saddest part of all.

I met Sara at a Quiznos, again another example of a typical thing typical people do on any typical day. Isn't that the most unlikely and uncommon place to meet the woman who takes your whole life, turns it upside down and shakes it like one of the snow globes with the winter scenes inside of it? But that was another way that she surprised me.

I wasn't even supposed to be at Quiznos that day, not that you're supposed to be anywhere at any given time I suppose, but that day, I was not supposed to be at that sandwich shop. I had gone to the hamburger stand, the one that's only open Memorial Day through Labor Day because the burgers are so good they do enough business in those three months to last them the rest of the year. They also do so much business that it's impossible for you to get a burger, or even a dog if that's your preference, unless you go at 11 a.m. and who wants to eat a burger that early in the morning? I always went at noon and took my chances. Sometimes I was lucky; sometimes I was not. That day, the day I first laid eyes on Sara, I was not. But as it turns out, that was the luckiest day of my life.

Graham, the guy who works with me, took one look at the line and shook his head.

"There's a long line," he said.

Graham was always doing that, stating the most obvious things. Because of this I'd taken to calling him Captain Obvious. Then, one day, it had been shortened to Captain. "Just like Captain Hook," he'd said and so now I called him Hook. Sometimes Captain Hook. Or sometimes just Captain.

He calls me Governor. He says he does it because I have so many opinions about so many things that I should run for office.

"You should, like, run for mayor or state rep or something,'" he said. "No, no. I got it. Governor. You should run for Governor."

And so it began. Either way, I never called him Graham and he never calls me Jaxson. It's just the way we do things. Some people would say Hook is my best friend. We work together and most nights, before I met Sara anyway, I was drinking beer at some bar watching some game while Hook flirted with some woman. We came and went freely in each other's homes; he knew how I took my coffee and always bought one for me on the way to pick me up for work, and when his dad had died, I'd been a pall bearer. So I guess if you add all those things together, multiply it by the number of hours a week we spend together and then subtract the number of hours we actually spend doing other things that would equal best friend capacity. But we never really talk about it much. Guys just don't do that.

Sara loved Hook, although it had taken her months to call him by that nickname.

"That's your thing with him," she said. And I had loved her more for not wanting to assume she was welcome into the weird world Hook and I had created for ourselves, even though she was.

"No fucking way we're getting burgers today," Hook said in that whiny kid voice he uses sometimes. "What the fuck are we going to eat?"

Let me interrupt here to tell you that we don't eat at Overton's more often than we do. They are just that freaking busy. So us not eating there wasn't as unexpected as Hook made it sound. And let me also say that there are about a dozen places to eat in the vicinity of Overton's. I know because I've eaten at all of them more times than I can count. Their napkins fill my glove box and are firmly entrenched in the seats of my truck.

I say this to make sure you understand that it was entirely possible that the day could have gone by without me meeting Sara just like hundreds of days had gone by before it. But that day was special. It was an accident, serendipity she would have called it.

On that day, I started rattling off some of those places but Hook just kept shaking his head.

"No, had that for dinner. No, had that Tuesday. No, remember how stale the bread was last time?"

I was getting tired of Hook's bullshit and was about to tell him to get the hell out of my truck and go find his own damn lunch when he said, "How about Quiznos?"

He had never asked to go to Quiznos before as it was clear across town and not near anything he and I ever need to be near. I state this because regardless of how it all ended, Hook was part of the reason I met Sara, him and the twenty-plus people greedily waiting for their Overton's burgers.

"Why do you want to go there for?" I asked. I state this so that you'll understand how little I had to do with the fact that I met Sara. Something greater than me was at work that day, call it God or whatever you want. I don't believe in God, but that's a story for another time. I can't write 'em all down, even though I could. I've got nothing but time now.

"I dunno. Try something new."

I hated when he did that. Usually he really liked routine. He wore the same boots to work for three and a half years before he stepped on a nail and the sole of the boot was so worn that it went through the rubber and caught his foot. But sometimes he did things like that day and wanted to drive to a bar three towns over "cuz we'd never been" or play Gin Rummy instead of Texas Hold 'Em because "everyone else plays Texas Hold 'Em."

I had stopped trying to rationale these sorts of things with Hook.

"Fucking Quiznos," I said and turned my pickup around. It whined and groaned at my desire to make it move so quickly and without notice.

Hook banged his hands against the interior of my car five times in quick succession.

"Fuckin' Quiznos!" he shouted.

I hadn't been happy about going to Quiznos. I couldn't believe it after I met Sara. I hadn't been happy about going to the place where she was going to be. That had never happened again since that day. Not once.

The line at Quizno's was much shorter and I had been thankful for that. Hook had jumped out of the car like an excited puppy.

"Fuckin' Quizno's!" he had shouted again and I just shook my head. Hook was like a kid brother to me sometimes, and, other times, he was the man I wanted to be when I grew up. It all depended on the day.

Hook hurried into line, more excited about a sandwich than any human being ever should be. I stood back a ways and read over the menu to decide what I wanted.

It was while I was pondering the menu that I heard the words that would change my life. You always imagine that words with that power will be profound, will give you the answers to ending world hunger or creating peace among warring factions. My life-changing words were: "Don't order the steak sandwich. The steak is really chewy, kinda like the consistency of a gummy bear."

I turned around and saw her. I didn't just see her, I later realized, but I saw me with her. I saw her and wanted to hold her face in my hands, run my fingers down her back to see if there was a key where you wound her up or if she was real.

Instead all I did was say, "Sounds pretty disgusting."

'It is. I had it Monday and I think I'm still trying to digest it."

I kept staring at her, not sure exactly what I should say but knowing that I should say something because this was no ordinary woman and this was no ordinary day. I knew that. You can say I'm crazy but it's the truth. Besides, this is my story and I can tell it anyway I want to. It's how I remember it that counts.

"Sorry," she said with a playful smile. "That's probably more information than you needed."

She had a nice smile. Not a closed-lip fake kind but one that showed her teeth and her teeth weren't all straight and white either. There was one that curled up a little and I immediately decided that all teeth should do this. It made her seem more real.

"What do you recommend?"

"Umm," she put a finger to her lip and thought for a minute. "The chicken club with smoked bacon is nice, if you like to mix your meats that is. The BBQ ribs are also surprisingly good but messy."

I looked down at my paint splattered shirt and torn jeans. "Don't suppose that'll be a problem for me. What do you think?"

She had laughed. "I suppose not."

"Thanks for the recommendation," I said. "I'll try that rib one you mentioned."

When it was my turn to order she hung back – "still making up my mind" she said – so I had time to lean in toward the cashier and tell him that I'd be paying for the sandwich of the woman behind me.

I paid for us both, and when I left, I just gave her a wave.

"Thanks again," I said. "Enjoy your lunch."

"Thanks. You too."

I got into the truck where Hook was already waiting for me and slowly pulled the door shut behind me. Then I slowly reached into the bag as if I was checking to make sure I had received the right sandwich.

"What're you doin'?" Hook asked. "Lose something in there?"

"Nope."

I continued to poke around.

"What the hell you doing Gov?"

"Nothing. Relax. Eat your sandwich."

Finally, just when I thought I'd run out of things to pretend to be looking for in my lunch bag I saw her coming out with a big grin on her face. She wagged an accusatory finger at me and came over to the driver's side of my car.

"Sneaky," she said.

"Actually, it's Jaxson," I said. "But you can call me…"

"Governor," Hook said with a toothy grin of his own. "He can call you…"

"Sara," she extended a hand and I took it. It was warm, but not sweaty. She didn't have fake fingernails. I liked that.

She stepped back and read the writing on the side of my truck: MacGregor Construction.

"This you?" she asked pointed to the name.

"Yep."

"Actually, it's his dad," Hook said as he pulled a pickle out from between the bread and dropped it into his mouth like trainer dropping a fish into the mouth of Shamu.

"It's me too," I said. "Why?"

"Well, I just moved into this old house and, well, it needs a lot of work. Honestly, I don't even know where to start."

"I could come by and take a look at it if you'd like," I said.

Hook had shut up because he knew that this was something he should not interrupt.

"Really? Would you?"

"Sure. Gimme your address."

I pulled a napkin out of the center console and handed it to her with a pen that was miraculously resting on the floor.

She wrote it down and handed to me with a smile.

"That's my address and number. Call me when you can come by and take a look?"

She said it like it was a question and I decided then that I wanted to spend the rest of my life being the answer to whatever she wanted to know.

So now you know about Sara. Well, you don't really know about her at all. You can't really because I'm not willing to share enough to let you know her, not the way I did. But don't worry. You'll know enough so that you can feel what I feel for her and understand what it was like when…well…I'll get to that.

I bet you're wondering about me. I recognize that the way I talk about Sara is not the way most men talk about most women. I've heard men describe women as "skirts" and "broads," "chicks" and "my old lady." I guess I used to be like that too. I remember back in the days before Sara, long before Sara, Hook and I would go out to bars, traveling hours away from home if need, be to find the perfect piece of "new ass." None of the women I met then really meant anything to me. If they were to read this, which they won't, I'm sure they'd say the same thing about me. I was just there, in the same place as they were at the same time and we both wanted to same thing, someone to be with when there was nothing but ice clinking around in the bottom of an empty glass and the bright lights of a soon to be closed bar shining on us telling us it was time to go home, alone or not.

They were all nice enough women. I don't mean to imply that they weren't. And they weren't whores, literally or figuratively. That's not my style. I never really understood the sort of guy who lays a woman nearly everyone he knows with a vowel in his name has laid already. Why? What's the sense? I always wanted sex, even if it was just a one or two night stand, to mean something. I would never have told that to my guy friends of course though Hook might have understood. He wasn't that kind of guy either far as I could tell.

Before Sara, there was one woman I dated for a long time. Her name was Evelyn and everyone, by that I mean the guys I work with, and of course Hook, thought that she was going to be the one to make an honest man out of me. But, I had to be honest with myself and admit that I didn't love this woman. I think she loved me and that made it even more important that I be honest and let her go. She was angry and probably had a right to be as I had let it go on for far too long and when she had hastily packed all her belongings, her favorite pair of jeans and sweet smelling bath soaps, into a box as she pushed away angry tears, she had looked at me long enough that it made me uncomfortable and want to turn away.

"I hope you find what you're looking for Jaxson," she staid. "I hope you find it before it's too late and you end up being lonely. That would be a shame."

I hadn't known until then that I was supposed to be looking for something but as soon as she said it I realized that she was right. I had wanted to tell her I was sorry but I wasn't sure how to apologize for something I hadn't realized I was doing wrong.

After her, it had taken me awhile to go back out and try to find someone. So long in fact that I still hadn't thought I was ready when Sara found me.

Anyway, I was telling you about me, wasn't I? It's easier to talk about other people. It's hard for me to talk about myself. I mean, you never describe yourself the way other people describe you. I think with most people, it's because they can't see their own faults. With me, it's all I can see.

So you already know that my name is Jaxson and that I work in construction and that for most of my life, I lacked something in myself that made it hard for me to connect with other people. I guess I could say that it was because of a lousy childhood, if it was in fact because of a lousy childhood, but I had a good childhood with good parents and siblings I actually liked a lot. Still do..

Anyway, I'm a guy's guy, whatever that means. At least that's what I've been told, by everyone except Sara.

"You're different than most men," she'd tell me after we made love and I held in my arms, caressing those shoulders, talking to her.

"How so?" I'd ask.

"Well, for one thing you're still awake," she'd joke. "And you're kind and compassionate and you want to know things about me."

"You're interesting," I told her.

So, to sum myself up, I guess I'd say that I'm a tough guy with a soft side that I didn't really realize was there until Sara. I like to work with my hands and I'm not a good cook. I prefer beer over wine and I don't really read anything that contains something longer than what can be read while I'm sitting on the john. I can fix most things that can go wrong with a car and I'm pretty good at household tasks and I like to sleep in on Saturdays. I can't carry a tune but I love country music, especially Kenny and Toby and Montgomery Gentry. I can't sit still for movies that are longer than two hours and really hate sequels because I don't like to wait to find out what happens.

I'm 43. And I'm the loneliest guy you'll ever meet. Or read about. I doubt we'll ever actually meet, but if we did, you'd see the loneliness. It's in my eyes. Even I can see that.

Most nights – Hook used to joke that it was all the days with a "y" at the end of it – I go to the Green Room and sit at the bar with my back to the door. In all those mob movies, the big boss guy never sits with his back to the door because he's afraid that someone will come in and off him and he'll never see the guy's face, not that it would matter much once he was dead anyway.

I order rum and coke and always take out that stupid little straw they give you that serves no purpose at all. I like it when the bartender gets a heavy hand and I can barely taste the coke. In fact, I appreciate that.

I had never wanted to be that guy who goes into a bar and people know your name, so I don't tell anyone my name. They call me the Governor, like Hook does, and they know just enough about me to buy me a free drink once in awhile. But nothing more. I only took Sara there once and then realized that she sparkled too much to be in a place so dark with the sorrows people were trying to drown, the stories that were so heavy with guilt that they made the air in the room so thick, it was hard to breathe. I never noticed it before Sara and I don't notice it after her. It is only by the contrast that you can see something like that.

After the night I took Sara there, I stopped going even though she had said she had a good time.

"It's a cute bar Jax," she said. "I can see why you like it. It has character."

I knew she meant it too. She wasn't just saying that. You could always count on Sara to speak the truth. It was one of about the six million things I loved about her. I know that's an exaggeration but please spare me the reminder. When you love someone like I love Sara, it's okay to exaggerate.

I'm now back at the Green Room every night. It's amazing how you revert to what you know, what you truly are maybe, when you lose what you thought you had and drop the façade of who you wanted to be.

No one said a word to me when I returned. They knew, of course, about all that had happened and they knew me well enough at least to know that I wouldn't want to talk about it, certainly not to them, and that it was best if they just left me alone, sitting with my back to the door, praying that someone would come in and start shooting so I could be put out of my misery.

The rum and coke drinks that I order are stronger now and when Drew remembers, he doesn't put the little straw in it. I appreciate these things because they are small little points of light in my now so dark and empty life. When you have nothing, you appreciate everything, even the things that meant nothing to you before.

I know you're probably wondering how the story is going to sort itself out. How I went from a guy who proposed to a woman wearing the perfect black dress in the middle of a dress shop on a Sunday afternoon to a guy who sits alone at a bar and is made happy by the absence of a small stick of plastic stuck into a glass. I'm getting to that part, but if you don't mind, I'd rather talk about the happy part for a little while longer. The only happiness I have is in the past so I like to think about it and talk about it when I can and today I have a captive audience in you, so please just stay with me for a little longer. The despair will come soon enough and then you'll wish you let me keep rambling about happier things.

Back to Sara.

After we met that day in Quiznos I did, in fact, go over to her house to see what work she needed done. I stepped out of my truck and stared at the house knowing that she had not been underestimating the amount of work it needed. She must have heard my truck coming up the gravel driveway, or else had been waiting for me which was what I told myself at the time, because she opened the door before I could mentally tally up restoration prices in my head. She was wearing a pair of cut-off jeans and a white tank top. She had a bandana on her head pulling her short hair off of her face. It was a Saturday.

"Hey you," she said. "Welcome to my most prized possession."

She swept her arm across the expanse of the house and I fell in love with her enthusiasm for this big, old, beautiful, decrepit house.

"What do you think?" she asked.

"Honestly?"

"Honestly."

"I think you've got a lot of work cut out for you."

"For us," she said.

The way she said it made something inside of me do something it had never done before. It's like when you move a piece of furniture that's been in the same spot for years and there are all those imprints on the carpeting from where it had embedded itself. It was like that.

"Oh yeah?" It was all I could think of to say.

"Well that's why you're here, silly," she said.

"That's not really why you're here," she said later over a dinner she cooked me while I was measuring and calculating, prodding and exploring the many rooms of her new home.

"Oh no?" I'd said as I paused with a forkful of string beans poised to go into my mouth.

"Nope."

"Why am I here, Sara?"

"You're here because I wanted to get to know you better. Because I think there is something more to you than meets the eye."

I hoped so. Not much met the eye as far as I was concerned. "What if I disappoint you?"

I hadn't thought about saying that before I said it and then after I did, I thought about how pathetic it sounded.

She had reached across the table and taken my hand and I realized that she was a woman who had, like me, spent time with people who she had wanted to care about but hadn't know how to. That she, like me, was ready for something more.

"You won't."

But I had. I had known at the time that I would, even though I had prayed to a God who, if I had been him, would have stopped listening to me years ago, that I wouldn't. I don't think she had known that I would though. That's the part that still stings. That's what wakes me up at night and makes me slam my fist into the empty pillow beside me, the one that used to hold her head of blond hair. Well, that and the loneliness is what wakes me up. Whoever knew that the absence of something could be so heavy that you could actually feel what was not there? I know now.

After that dinner, it had been Sara and me, me and Sara for a stretch of time that seems now impossible to calculate in days and weeks, even months and years. A year to the day of meeting in Quiznos, we got married. It had seemed silly to me at first, to be 36 and planning a wedding complete with bridesmaids and groomsmen. But it was what Sara wanted; "You only do this once, Jax," she said in a phrase that should have felt foreboding at the time but hadn't. Sara was just 30 then and so color schemes and flower arrangements had meant something to her and I wasn't going to minimize anything that mattered. She deserved to be, as she said, a pretty, pretty princess for a day.

Sara had pretty friends and Hook and the other boys I work with, along with my brother Teddy and brother-in-law Mark weren't bad looking guys either, so our wedding was aesthetically pleasing and also, I am told, a lot of fun. I barely remember it. I remember staring at Sara and thinking that there was no way she was mine. She'd catch me watching her and she'd blush. Then she'd mouth "I love you" and I would feel tears in my eyes and realize that I had found what I had been missing, the something that Evelyn had noticed wasn't there long ago. And I was thankful.

They say that after you get married, things go down hill, at least for the guy. The sex becomes more infrequent, the cutesy things your wife did become annoying and the things you like to do with your buddies become replaced by things your wife likes to do. But not with Sara. Things got better, though I hadn't thought that was possible.

Sara wasn't like other women.

"I don't want you to stop being who you are," she said when I'd casually mention that Hook wanted to go for a drink that night after work.

Other women had said it before but Sara really meant it. She'd leave notes for me on the kitchen table if she went to bed before I got home that said: Hope you had fun with Graham. I watched a chick flick and drank wine straight out of the bottle (see empty bottle in sink as proof.) Come join me in bed – I missed you. Love, S.

And I'd happily climb into bed next to the first woman who understood me and loved me anyway.

It's ironic that it was a night like that when everything went horribly wrong. I always thought it was funny when people said things like that, as if there are good ways for things to go wrong. I guess it is just meant to emphasize how bad things can get, worse than just wrong. I'm going to put off telling you for just a little bit longer. And when I do tell you I promise to try and make it quick and painless, at least for you, like one of those shots they give you at the doctor's and tell you it'll only hurt for a minute. I won't labor over all the sad points and won't try to describe the sort of agony I lived through, if you can call what I do living. I'll just tell you and leave it at that. I won't want to write anymore after I tell you anyway. I'll need to be alone. I hope you understand.

Sara and I lived in my house until we finished working on hers, a task that took almost two years to complete. When we finally moved in, we spent the first night lying on the floor of the living room looking up at the stained glass window we had installed.

"It's beautiful, isn't it?" she said with a sigh in her voice that gave me a shiver.

"It is. Great idea babe. I never would have thought of…"

"No," she said, turning on her side to face me. "I mean our life. It's beautiful. I am in love with our life."

I had turned my head toward her and she ran her hand down my cheek.

"I love you Jaxson MacGregor."

Then she kissed me and just like the hundreds of times before, I felt like I was living in a dream and I was waiting for someone to pinch me and have this all fade away and I'd be lying on my own bed, in my own house, alone. Sara would be just a dream. I wondered about this as we started to make love, until I let myself get carried away by her.

In the end it wasn't a pitch, it was a high-pitched squeal and an unearthly cry that tore me out of my fantasy world. I'm ready to tell you the story now. Like I said, I'm going to try and get it over with quickly so hold on. Once I start, I can't slow down. And don't try to console me if I get all emotional while I tell you. I can't be consoled. I'm learning to live with that.

The night things went wrong was a night like so many nights before. Sara and I had just finished dinner and we were cleaning up.

"Go ahead. I'll finish," she said as she grabbed a plate out of my hand.

"It's okay," I said. "Hook can wait. Let me at least help you."

She smiled and pulled harder on the plate.

"No really. It's okay. You're already late. I got this. It won't be much work."

I waited until she put the dish in the dishwasher and then I grabbed her tight around the waist.

"I love you," I said.

She turned around and hugged me.

"I know. Now get outta here. Say hi to Graham."

I left thinking, as I often did, how lucky I was to have Sara.

I got to the bar and still felt happy. Hook usually called it my shit-eating grin and he did that night too.

"Sara got a sister?" he asked as he so often did.

"Yes, but she's married," I said as I so often did.

To an outside observer Hook, and I probably seem like actors in a play or characters on a television show. We have our parts, we play them well, and the script always seems predictable, even to us. I'd sort of outgrown Hook in some ways since Sara. I hadn't meant to but he just didn't understand what wedded bliss was all about and I was still trying to figure it out for myself. In the three years since I'd known Sara, she and I had gone on several double dates with Hook and several different women and we had learned never to get to know any of them too well. Sara had tried at first to make each feel welcome into our little circle since most of them were younger than us and much more nervous. But after awhile, even her goodwill had worn off and she'd been polite but nothing more. "At least not until the third date," she'd said. Rarely did that come.

Hook was younger than me and had been further behind mentally the entire time we'd been friends, but I hadn't really noticed until Sara. He was still my best friend but it had gotten harder and harder to talk to him because our lives were so different now. I know he felt it too and so when we were together, I tried to pretend like everything was the same. Even though we both knew it wasn't.

When we left that night, after a few hours of drinks and a disappointing loss in a string of disappointing losses by the New York Jets, Hook shook my hand, something he'd never done before and said, "You look good, Gov. Married life is treating you well."

It was his acknowledgement, I realized later, of the fact that he did realize we were now living our separate lives and that he was okay with it as long as I was happy.

I shook his hand firmly.

"Thanks, man. I hope you get to find out what it feels like one day."

He laughed and punched me with his free arm.

"Nah, like a drifter, I was born to walk alone," he said with a smile.

I laughed.

"See you at work tomorrow, man."

"See you. Cuz here I go again on my own."

"You okay to drive?"

I always asked and he always said yes. It was a guy thing.

We parted ways and I went home to a note from Sara and some middle of the night sex. It was always good even when she was sleepy.

It wasn't until the next morning when I got to work and Hook wasn't there that things in my life stopped being so good. I thought at first that he was just hung over and sleeping in so I covered for him with the other guys until about 11 a.m. when it was well past the time he would have arrived, even if he was hungover. I waited until noon and then went to his house. His truck wasn't there and I knew immediately that he hadn't made it home last night. There was this woman – what was her name? – that he had been spending a lot of time with lately. Damn. *Think*, I told myself. Jessica? Jaime? Janice? Yes, Janice. I didn't remember much about her except that she worked at the hair salon Sara went to. I drove there. She was surprised to see me.

"Hi, Gov," she said with a smile, obviously not applying Sara's rule of inside jokes even though she had only met me twice before.

"Hi Janice," I said wondering how to ask what I was about to ask. "Have, uh, have you seen Hook?"

"Recently?" she asked.

"Yeah. Like last night."

She shook her head of black hair.

"No. We're supposed to go out tonight. Why? He skip out on work or somethin'?"

"Yeah. Somethin'."

I drove to the hospital and explained who I was to the emergency room nurse. Her thin-lipped expression was further confirmation of what I knew to be true. I wasn't surprised when she led me down a hall to a room that held Hook, or what was left of him, in a bed of wires and tubes. I only had to look at him once to know that he wasn't really there anymore. Hook, at least the one I'd known, was far away from that hospital bed. I hoped that wherever he was, he was happy.

I won't go into all the details of having to call Hook's family and tell them what had happened to him or of them flying out from Michigan to make the decision about taking him off the life support. I won't talk about the funeral or the eulogy his mother had asked me to give. I won't talk about how it wasn't until after he died that I realized Janice might have loved him and he might have finally been on the way to having what he didn't think he was ever going to have. I won't talk about the way I holed myself up in my room and didn't go to work for two whole weeks because it was simply too empty at the construction site without him.

Do I have to tell you that I blame myself for Hook's death? I blame myself for pushing him aside, like an old suit goes to the back of the closet when you buy a new one. I blame myself for never saying out loud to him that he was my best friend. I blame myself for letting him drive home the last night we were together when I'd watch him drain glass after glass of beer. He'd hit a telephone pole. Had he seemed that drunk, or had I been too busy thinking about making love to Sara to notice if he slurred his words or swayed on his walk to his truck?

At first Sara was patient. Actually, to be fair, she was patient for a long time. She held me and cried with me and soothed me in every way she could think of. She mourned with me because she had loved Hook. She stayed home with me the entire first week doing nothing but sitting with me in bed, petting my head like I was a child home sick from school. She held my hand during the funeral and helped me write the eulogy. She was patient to a point that was hard to comprehend and I wanted to thank her for it but never really did. I was too busy feeling sorry for myself.

After a week, Sara went back to work and I still stayed home. The feelings of guilt were worse when Sara wasn't there to hold me and I let my mind run away with all the ways I had killed Hook slowly each day more painfully than the blow of the telephone pole. Whether Hook really cared that much about the chasm in our friendship, I don't know but when I thought about it when I was alone, he did care. He cared so much that he had been thinking about it while he was driving and that had been the distraction that caused him to drive off the road.

Please don't. Don't tell me that it's not my fault. Don't look at me with those eyes of sympathy. I don't deserve it and, hell, I don't want it. So please, just keep listening but whatever you do, don't feel sorry for me.

It was months after Hook's death that Sara tried to breath life back into me. One night she turned to me and ran her hand down my chest, a signal that she wanted to make love. I rolled to my other side, my back to her. It wasn't that I didn't want to make love to her but just that I didn't think I deserved to feel good.

"Jax," she whispered into my ear. "I want us to make a baby."

I shook my head against the pillow.

"No," I said.

"Come on, Jax. You said that when we finished the house we could try. I want to try. I'm getting older and..."

"No, Sara," I said. "No."

It wasn't that I didn't want to make a baby with Sara but that I didn't trust myself with one.

And so in the end, I denied Sara the thing she wanted most and it was something she couldn't live without. Telling a woman you will not give her a child is like no other denial that exists. I learned that.

I started going back to the Green Room and ordering my rum and cokes, minus the straw, and sitting with my back to the door and watching other people around me talk about lives I could not understand because I no longer really had one. When I'd come home late, there were no more notes for me on the kitchen table and when I slept in to nurse my hangover, she left the house without saying goodbye.

She continued to be patient and to try and help me through my grief, but when she turned 35 and I still would not budge on the subject of a child, I knew the end was near. When she asked for a divorce, I was not surprised. When I said that I'd give it to her, she cried.

"Why are you crying?" I'd asked. "It's what you wanted."

"Why, of all the things I want, is this the one you decide to give me?" she cried.

I'll never forget those words for as long as I live, which I don't think will be too long. Although I'm not sure. You can never really tell those sorts of things.

On the day that I left, she used Evelyn's words: "I hope you find what will make you happy Jax." But she added a special twist: "I wish that I could have given it to you. I love you enough to do it."

She had gotten down on her knees then and held my hands up to her face which was drenched with tears.

"Please, tell me what to do and I'll do it. We can stop all of this if you want to. Just tell me what to do."

And then I had said the words that I will regret until my dying day. Whenever that is.

"Just let me leave, Sara," I told her.

And so she had and now the perfect dress that once belonged to the perfect woman hangs in the closet of my tiny apartment. She had packed it among my things with a note pinned to it that said: I could never wear this for anyone but you.

So there you have it. Do you think I am a pathetic soul who was so torn apart by the death of a friend that he lost what mattered to him? Or do you think I'm an ignorant asshole who not once, but twice, disappointed the people closest to him? I don't really care which one it is. I have my own opinions of myself.

That a guy like me could love a woman like her and then be stupid enough to do something to lose her could mean that the entire world is doomed to failure because there are certainly plenty of other stupid men like me.

But that perfect black dresses exist for women who deserve to feel beautiful and that love can and do exist for those who know what to do with then might mean that there is hope for salvation.

But I don't see it that way.

And it's my story. I'll tell it how I want to.

A COLD NIGHT IN MAUI

~*~

A.J. O'Connell

Author's Notes: The inspiration from this story came from Comrade, the only man I know who calls in sick to his favorite bar. In fact, Comrade is the only man I know who wears a fedora, or even owns one. Such a distinctive person merits his very own story, so none of the other players make a cameo in this piece. Like the man himself, the story is short, and sweet.

~*~

I was working late one night in my office when this dame comes in. She was the kind of woman you couldn't forget if you'd had a lobotomy. She had dark hair, dark eyes and a mustache that would make Fidel Castro jealous. She was shaped like a potato.

I love potatoes.

She looked as if she had been crying.

"Vladmir Illyanovich?" she asked in an accent that made my toes curl first one way then the other. "You are... you are private eye?"

"That's right, sweetheart," I says to her. "Sit down. Make yourself comfortable."

She moved to take a seat, her drab skirt clinging to her curves like a burlap bag. As she passed by me, I caught her scent: fried sausage and cheap vodka. This was my kind of broad.

"Oh Vladimir," she says, pulling the three-corned scarf from her head, "I need help. My name is Svetlana Petrova. My husband, he cheat on me with.... capitalist. When he come home he smell like..." she made a noise like a broken toilet, "Like new car and perfume."

"Don't worry, doll," I says to her, handing her a standard-issue handkerchief and a glass of Smirnoff. "Tell me everything."

She mopped her eyes and blew her nose and mopped her eyes again.

"It start two months ago - my husband Ivan, he is not home from work on time. He say he work late – for union – and I believe. My Ivan, very good worker. But then he come home with... lipstick on collar.

"Oh Vlad," she says, draining her glass. "Your uncle Karl say you help me. Your uncle say," she poured another and poured it into herself, "you are best communist private eye in Maui."

"Well," I tell her, pulling my fedora down on my forehead and adjusting the collar of my blue-collar Hawaiian shirt, "I do know a thing or two about enemies of world workers' unity."

"I know," she sobbed. "I know. I would not come to you if she were not... capitalist pig. I fear worst, Vladimir. I fear she is..." she reached for the Smirnoff's again. I pushed it towards her, "I fear she is CEO. I fear she is... union buster!"

I've seen a couple of things in my time, but this made even *my* flesh crawl.

The idea of some big-haired, red power-suited, high-heeled capitalist floozy, corrupting an honest comrade while disbanding the very union that fed his family, made me see red.

I stood up. The desk chair ricocheted against the wall.

"Where is he, Svetlana?" I asked, taking my pistol from my desk drawer. "Bring me to him."

Sniffling, she led me through the streets of Maui, until we came to a club that sparkled at the side of the road like diamonds on a whore.

She led me inside. In an instant I could see that it was the sort of place where old world men from the U.S.S.R. played new world games, dressed in Miami Vice white suits and Chips black sunglasses; chest hair billowing over the collars of tight pastel tee shirts while they chased their Coca Cola dreams.

The idea of Ivan and his executive tramp carousing here made me sick.

"That's him," a man screamed in Russian. "That's Karl's nephew! Get him."

The guns came out. I drew my piece but it was too late.

I looked over to Svetlana for help, but she was stripping away her drab blue housedress to reveal a slinky red sequined number the size of a small tarp.

The last thing I saw before everything went black was a Hawaiian shirt and the barrel of a revolver.

"Dames," I thought, as I bled out on the carpet. "You just can't trust 'em."

CARLOTTA'S GIFT

~*~

N. Apythia Morges

Author's Notes: The inspiration from this story came mainly from the Banker but minor characters and events were also inspired by Carlos, The Comrade, and Thomas James Kane.

~*~

Carlotta gripped the bedpost as her father tightened the laces of her corset. She bit her lip to hold back tears caused not by the unpleasant digging of the boning into her young skin but by what the corset meant. Her father was expecting her to perform her other duties tonight.

While she usually joined the other women for a dance and sometimes a song at her father's club, Pièce Verte, there would be occasions when her father wanted something badly enough or owed someone a debt he couldn't afford that he would offer his only daughter up as payment.

One would think that in the civilized year of 1953, these things no longer happened. But not all of the French had made a swift recovery from the horrors of war. Some of the lower classes found that survival in a war-torn nation meant reverting to uncivilized dealings. It was that same attitude that kept her father's business afloat in the worst of times; even the poor craved wine and women. And everyone knew that Monsieur Boisvert had a cure for every itch, legal or not.

"There," said her father as he knotted the lace. "Let me look at you."

She dropped her hands to her side and stepped away from the bed. Any shame she might have felt at having her own father dress her in red silk panties, corset, silk stockings with matching gloves and stilettos died a long time ago. It had been nearly two years since the first time he came into her room bearing such a costume. The events of those two years made Carlotta feel much older than her sixteen years. She briefly thought about how mortified her mother would be to see her like this. Shaking her head, she pushed those thoughts aside. Her mother was long dead and could not help her now. Only her submission to her father's will would keep her from being tied to the bedpost and beaten.

"*Ma petite*, you look stunning as always," he said. "You will make me proud tonight and listen to Monsieur Lesage."

It was an order rather than a question, but she answered anyway, her voice reflecting her resignation to her fate. "Of course papa. As you wish."

"Good. Now get downstairs."

The Pièce Verte was situated in a warehouse that had been abandoned during the war. Her father scavenged other desolate buildings in search of salvageable furnishing, and what he couldn't find, he looted. Eventually, he found financial backers, stern Eastern Bloc soldiers remaining in France after their service who found his idea of a club to fulfill the needs of men titillating.

Not one to waste money, her father insisted they live above the club in a cramped room large enough for two beds, a small sofa, and a sink in the corner. All food was prepared in the club's kitchen.

Poverty and desperation were all Carlotta knew. The only splurges her father allowed were for the expensive lingerie he dressed her in when the need arose and his own finely tailored suits that he wore at the club. Any profits not spent on garments were usually wasted on any one of her father's vices.

Notions of privacy and morality weren't part of her upbringing. Her mother had died too early to instill them on her daughter, and her father thought of her as a means to an end and nothing more, so the idea that a teenage girl should have her own room never crossed his mind.

She didn't hate her life; on the contrary, she thought it rather fun most of the time. Because she did not attend school nor did she didn't have friends her own age, she didn't have a basis for comparison as to what a "normal" girl her age did. She spent her nights in the club doing whatever her father asked. Some nights she cooked, others she served drinks, and the best nights were when she got to fill in and sing and dance as part of the floor show.

She learned skills on the job. She found the women there fascinating, and, sometimes, they would take pity on her and give her lessons in everything from English to sewing. They took to Carlotta as if she were their communal daughter, and they were the closest thing she had to a mother. If they disagreed with a child being part of the act, they never said a word. Though they loved Carlotta, their own need for survival was far greater, and there was not much work available for unskilled women these days, unless one wanted to spend long days doing back-breaking manual labor to earn what these woman made in one hour on their backs without breaking a sweat. No, they would love Carlotta, but they would not stand up for her. Not tonight.

These nights were the times that she hated her life. While dancing, she could pretend she was a famous starlet and that the men had traveled the world just to see her. But what fantasy could she invoke when she was forced to lay on a bed and allow a bestial stranger to take liberties with her body?

She loved her Papa, even though he was the one to put her in this situation. After all, he was all that she had. If she behaved and did as she was told, he would grant her a rare smile and allow her to spend the rest of the night upstairs reading. If not… Well she didn't want to think about that.

The first and only time she refused to follow her Papa's orders was the second time he had dressed her. She had known what that meant, and she wanted no part of it. He backhanded her, sending her sprawling on the floor, where she lay shocked and horrified. Dragging her over to the bed, he had used one of her long gloves to tie her hands behind the post and removed his belt. It was nearly six weeks before the marks had faded.

Standing outside the door to the club, she took a deep breath. She felt herself fade away to that special place inside. A place that protected the little girl she once was and whatever innocence she may have left. When she let out the breath, nothing remained except sheer will to do what needed to be done. She opened the door.

Monsieur Lesage finished buckling his belt before reaching out to ruffle Carlotta's long, black hair. "You truly are a beauty," he said, leaning in to kiss her one more time.

She allowed him to possess her mouth, knowing in a few moments he would be gone, and she could escape upstairs.

"Your father underestimates your value." He looked at her with something close to compassion masquerading in his eyes. She figured it was a mask because anyone who would agree to bed another's young daughter as debt repayment wouldn't understand a word such as compassion.

He reached into his pocket and withdrew some francs that he placed in her hand. "You take this and hide it, *Mon Cherie*. You are almost of age and will not have to be your father's bargaining chip much longer."

Carlotta said nothing. He was not the first man to try to bribe his way out of a guilty conscience. They never understood how insulting the money was, how it only made her feel like more of a whore.

Monsieur Lesage sighed. "May we meet on better terms some day, *Mon Cherie*." With a tip of his head, he left the room.

She waited until she was sure he would not be returning before sliding out from under the sheets. Slipping on the robe that hung on the back of the door, she gathered up her clothing and exited the room.

One end of the warehouse had been portioned off to allow for the creation of six rooms that held nothing but a bed and a nightstand with a lamp. These rooms were where the women of Pièce Verte truly made their money. This was the part of the club Carlotta hated. She hung her head as she walked, sounds of wooden headboards banging against concrete walls as men's moans filled the dimly lit hallway. She nodded to Gerard who guarded the last doorway, but couldn't meet his eyes. He stepped aside and gave her access to the back stairway that would take her up to her home where she would spend the next hour in a hot bath scrubbing off Monsieur Lesage's compassion.

The pounding on the door grew louder as Carlotta ran across the club to open it. It was only three and the club didn't open until six. Knowing only someone who had dealings with her father would be that persistent, she hesitated before opening the door.

A big, muscular man she had never seen shoved the door a side, pushing her roughly in the process. "Where is Tomas?" he demanded.

"My father is out."

"Out screwing another man's wife, is he?" He searched the room as if he expected to see her Papa walk out at the sound of this accusation.

She was frightened by the look of fury in the man's eye. He turned on her like a wild dog, and she feared what he might do. "Where is he?"

"I don't know," she said quickly. "He does not tell me his business."

"Your father is not here." A feral grin spread across his face. She shivered as his voice dropped to a cold whisper as he reached out and grabbed her arm, pushing her back into the room. "When will he be back?"

"I don't know." She squirmed, trying to free herself from his grip. He only tightened his hold.

"I hear stories that your father uses you to pay his debts."

She said nothing.

He looked her over as one might examine a piece of livestock. "Yes, it is only fitting. A daughter for a wife."

Before she knew what was happening, the man hit her, knocking her to her knees. "So eager?" he jeered as he unbuckled his belt.

"No! Please don't," she whimpered, backing away.

He lashed out at her with the belt. Instinctively, she put up her hands. Her mind filled with the memory of her father's beating, freezing her in fear. She did nothing as the man took the belt and tied her hands together. It was only when he pushed her onto her back that she began to scream for him to stop.

"That's it, little girl," he whispered in her ear as he lay on top of her. "Scream for me."

It was Marietta, one of the kitchen staff, who found her hours later huddled in a dark corner, her shredded dress and haunting eyes telling the story Carlotta could not. Marietta gathered the girl into her arms and whispered prayers to the Virgin Mother on her behalf.

Carlotta awoke later to find herself in a bed. She knew by the softness of it that it was not her own. Opening her eyes, she saw Marietta watching her from a chair next to the bed.

"Hello child," she whispered.

Carlotta tried to speak but her mouth hurt to move.

"Don't," Marietta gently urged her. "You have taken quite a beating as well as..." She averted her eyes, leaving the sentence hanging; Carlotta needed no reminder of what had happened.

"My father..." she started, but the words came out as nothing more than a whisper.

"He knows what happened and that you are here. You are to stay here until you are well."

Carlotta missed the rest of what Marietta said as she gave over to the comforting nothingness of sleep.

The two weeks Carlotta spent with Marietta and her husband, Palmroy Rousseau, were some of the happiest times in her life. She spent the days talking to Marietta as they did the washing she took in as well as baking. Monsieur Rousseau, in turn, would spend evenings reading the daily newspaper with Carlotta, educating her about world events while Marietta was at the club. It was like being part of a real family, something Carlotta was beginning to regret not having experienced.

As soon as Carlotta was able to walk without pain again and the angry red cuts around her wrists scabbed over, her father demanded that she come home. She was needed to help in the kitchen since one of the staff quit. Although she wanted nothing more than to remain with the Rousseaus, she was still too weak to withstand another beating, so she obediently followed him home.

She barely saw her Papa during the next few weeks, and when they did end up in the same space, he looked at her with such disgust that she would immediately avert her eyes and leave the room. She wondered what made him look at her like that. He couldn't possibly hold her responsible for what had happened, could he? She asked Marietta about it the next day.

"It is guilt, child. That look is not for you but for what your Papa is feeling. He knows that you have paid for his sins, for his indiscretion with Monsieur Riffaud's wife," Marietta told her as she and Carlotta kneaded the bread dough.

"He has used me to repay his debts for years without guilt. Why is this different?"

"Because, child, he has convinced himself that you do his bidding willingly. This time, it was not your choice."

Somewhere during the last seven weeks, Marietta had become a substitute mother for Carlotta, and Carlotta decided to be brave and confide the truth to the older woman.

"It was never willingly, Marietta. But what choice did I have? I did as he said, or I got beaten. Sex might wound my pride and fill me with shame, but those wounds are easier to hide."

"They are also sometimes more painful," Marietta said wisely. Carlotta averted her eyes.

"Stop that," Marietta said, raising Carlotta's chin. "You haven't done anything wrong. Do not carry the burden of other's guilt."

Tears welled up in Carlotta's eyes. "I don't want to do this anymore, Marietta," she whispered.

The older woman wrapped her arms around the young girl, gently rubbing her back. "We will find a way out for you, child. I promise."

Carlotta woke up the next morning feverish with a sore throat. She groaned as her aching body protested being moved out of bed. Her father was long gone and in his place was a list of chores she was expected to finish by the time he returned. She gave one last longing look at her bed before gathering up the laundry and carrying it down the stairs.

By the time Marietta arrived, Carlotta had noticed blister-like lesions on her palms. She assumed it was from the wooden mop handle and worked faster so that she could end the torment. It was Marietta's gasp that made her look up.

Marietta was at her side, grabbing her shoulders and staring intently at Carlotta's face, her eyes widening in surprise. "Oh child," she whispered in a sad way that made Carlotta nervous.

"What is it?"

"How do you feel?" Marietta asked, ignoring Carlotta's question.

"I woke up feeling ill. I think I am getting the flu."

Marietta's face filled with a look of regret. "Not the flu child."

"Then what?"

"Come, up to bed with you. I'll call for the doctor."

"Marietta, what is it? Why are you acting like this?"

"Let the doctor answer your questions child. Now off to bed."

"But the floors.."

"Leave them."

Carlotta obeyed.

Dr. Morel was a small man of a questionable background, but he was discrete and willing to make house calls, which made him a favorite among the Pièce Verte crowd. He barely spent five minutes examining Carlotta before stepping back from her bed.

"You were right, Mrs. Rousseau. She does, in fact, have syphilis," he said.

"What?" Carlotta cried in dismay, trying to get out of bed.

"Shh," cooed Marietta. "It will be all right."

"Here." Dr. Morel shoved a piece of paper into Marietta's hand. "Make sure she takes the pills as directed. They will help with the lesions."

"Am I going to die?" Carlotta asked in a small voice.

"Everyone dies," said the doctor with a shrug.

Both women gasped.

"But this will not kill you now. You still have years ahead of you." He pulled his coat on before bidding the two good day.

Carlotta turned her horror-filled eyes to Marietta, who pulled her close.

"Don't listen to that nasty man, child. You will live a long, happy life."

Carlotta wanted to believe her, but she couldn't.

"I will go out and get the pills now. You rest," Marietta ordered.

Carlotta nodded and laid back down. It wasn't long before she fell into a fitful sleep.

"Carlotta!" Her father's angry voice traveled up the stairs. "Get your useless self down here!"

She tried to get out of bed but was too weak to stand. She collapsed helplessly back onto the mattress, not even having the energy to shout to him. Even if she did, she didn't think her throat would allow her to.

She listened as her father stormed up the stars and threw the door open.

"Didn't you hear me?" he roared. "How dare you disobey me? Answer me."

She tried to protest but her voice was a whisper that got lost in her father's tirade. She saw him remove his belt and felt her muscles tense, awaiting the blow.

"Tomas! What are you doing?" Marietta had entered the room, situating herself between him and his daughter. "You will not beat her for being ill!"

"Ill?" he said sneering in disbelief.

"Look at her!"

Her father's gaze took in Carlotta. Recognition lit in his eyes. "You little whore!" he screamed, raising the belt again.

"Tomas!"

"Papa!"

"How dare you? Who was it?" he demanded, advancing on Carlotta.

Carlotta simpered, huddled up on the bed to protect herself from her Papa's insults as well as his blows.

Marietta stood her ground against Tomas. "Tomas Boisvert! You know who is responsible for this! Why this happened to her."

At once, the anger fled his body. He bowed his head. Silence descended on the room. Raising his head, he glared at Carlotta. "Get out."

"What Papa?"

"Get out. You are of no use to me anymore. I have been punished enough in this lifetime. Leave."

With that, he strode out of the room, slamming the door.

Carlotta looked at Marietta in disbelief. She was being disowned. She was ill. Where would she go? She clung to Marietta.

"Don't worry child. You will come stay with me. We will worry about this when you are well."

Marietta began to gather Carlotta's belongings into bags. "We will take only what you need. I will call Palmroy. He'll help you walk. I know it will be difficult child, but will you try?"

Carlotta nodded. Though her future was uncertain, knowing that the Rousseaus weren't abandoning her made the thought bearable.

"There is money," she said, though the effort was painful.

"What do you mean?"

"Francs from the men…" Carlotta couldn't finish the sentence.

"It will be alright, child."

"In the box."

The music box was the only memento she had of her mother. Marietta slid it into the bag with Carlotta's clothes. "All will be well child."

After another week in Marietta's care, Carlotta was restored to good health. The medicine had cleared up the lesions and the flu symptoms were gone. Walking out into the tiny kitchen, she took a seat at the table and watched Marietta peel potatoes.

"What will happen to me now?" she asked.

Marietta gently put down the knife and wiped her hands on her dishtowel. "You know you are welcome to stay here, but your Papa –"

"I know. He will fire you if I stay."

"I can find another job."

"No, Marietta, you and Monsieur Rousseau have done more than enough for me. I will not have you lose income because of me. I will go. I've learned enough working the club to be of use to someone."

"There is another option."

"What is that?"

"I have a cousin in Algeria. He owns a vineyard near the village of Aïn Merane, near Algiers. I wrote to him months ago when, well, when you were here last time and told him of your plight."

Carlotta looked down, blushing that her potential new employer knew her seedy past.

"What did I tell you about that, child?" Marietta said sternly.

Carlotta raised her eyes.

"That is better," Marietta said.

"He said he would hire you on to help out," she continued. "You could teach the workers French, help mind the children and tend to some cooking and cleaning. His wife is very ill, and he could use another woman's presence. Think of it as being a governess.

"If you want the position, he will pay for your trip down. You would take the train to Marseilles and then a boat to Algiers where he would meet you."

Carlotta looked out the window. Algeria. She knew nothing of the place. She was frightened at the prospect of going so far away. Yet she knew she couldn't stay with Marietta. She wouldn't repay her kindness in such a way. And what would happen to her if she remained in France? She knew her future would consist of either factory work or prostitution. Neither sounded appealing.

"Think of it as an adventure, child." Marietta said gently. "You can start over. No one will know your past. You can create your own destiny."

Carlotta offered her a weak smile; she didn't believe in destiny. Knowing that Marietta had gone out of her way to help, Carlotta found herself agreeing to flee the country in hopes of finding happiness in a foreign land.

As the ship approached the port, Carlotta was in awe of the city before her. A wall of white, multistory buildings seemed to rise out of the sea to meet her, the curtains of the many windows winking at her in the breeze. Even more houses crowded up the hills. There was something reassuring in their sameness. The place looked welcoming; while it was obviously a big city, it had an airy, open feel that was lacking in France's major metropolitan areas.

When she disembarked, she was greeted by a handsome blond man with a dark tan. He had a little girl of about two in his arms and two boys who looked to be about five and seven huddled around his legs.

"You must be Carlotta," he said warmly, offering a hand.

"Jean St. James?" she asked, taking his hand.

"The one and the same. And this beautiful girl is Claudia. That" he pointed to the five year old, "is James. And this strapping lad is Pierre."

"How do you do?" Carlotta said, shaking each of the boys' hands.

"And this is Messali Abbas," he gestured to the gentleman who had claimed her trunk. "He is the manager of our operations. The vineyard would surely fall apart without him."

"Hello Monsieur Abbas," Carlotta said, extending her hand to the dark man with striking features and a strong build.

"Please, call me Messali." He kissed the back of her hand the way the upper-class French gentlemen did.

She blushed and lowered her eyes. "Thank you for finding my trunk."

"My wife sends her apologies for not being here to greet you, but she was not up to traveling," said Jean.

Marietta had told her that Madame St. James had breast cancer and most likely would not last the year. That was why Monsieur St. James was most eager to take in a stranger for a governess; he wanted his wife to know that her children would be cared for in her absence.

"Your wife's health is more important, Monsieur St. James," she said.

"If you are to call Messali by his given name, than you shall do the same with me. After all, you are part of our family now."

"Thank you, Jean." She smiled warmly.

"Daddy, I wanna go home to mommy," Claudia said.

"And so we shall, my dearest. The car is that way," he said, taking off toward the parking lot.

"Now Claudia, would you be a sweetheart and allow Mademoiselle Boisvert to hold you during the ride?"

Claudia narrowed her eyes at Carlotta as if trying to decide whether or not her lap was worthy. Finally she nodded. Carlotta held out her arms, and Claudia situated herself on Carlotta's lap.

"Mademoiselle Bo.. Boo...." James was trying to talk to her.

"You may call me Carlotta," she said.

"Mademoiselle Carlotta," Jean corrected from the front seat. "We always talk to adults with respect." He winked at Carlotta in the rear view mirror. She smiled slightly. No one had acknowledged her as an adult before. It made her feel proud and want to prove herself worthy of the title.

"Mademoiselle Carlotta," James said, "Do you know how to jump rope?"

"Yes I do, James." He looked impressed. "Do you?"

"No, but Pierre is trying to teach me. Sometimes he is too busy learning to ride his bike to help me though." He shot Pierre a glare.

"I would be more than happy to teach you to jump rope, James," she assured him. That seemed to make the child happy.

The rest of the car ride to Aïn Merane was filled with general get-to-know you talk. Jean was the third-generation owner of the vineyard. He was also co-owner of a winery in France that had been in the family for nearly 100 years. When his father died, Jean stayed to run the farm, and his younger brother took over the daily operations of the winery.

Messali was a second-generation farm manager. His father, a native Algerian, had been the previous overseer, and Messali worked his way up to management, just as his father had. He knew all the inner workings of the vineyard and was obviously held in high esteem by Jean. Their mutual respect was apparent.

As they rode on, Jean outlined a generalization of what Carlotta's day would be like. She would wake with the children and get the boys to school. She would spend time playing and instructing Claudia as well as taking care of the household duties. Three evenings a week, she would offer French lessons to any of the employees who wished to learn. On Sundays, she would accompany the family to church and make the house presentable to receive guests afterward. Saturdays would be her own.

The car drove up a dirt road that ended at a sprawling house with white walls, much like those along the seafront. A small stone porch trailed around the corner. Surrounding it were vast fields of green vine and dark grape that eventually ended in the rising mountains. Everything was lush and alive. "It's beautiful," she whispered, taking in the spectacular view.

"I'm glad you like it. It is your home now, too."

James stopped the car, and the children hurriedly exited, running toward the porch door. James turned in his seat to face Carlotta as did Messali.

"Carlotta, I wanted to speak to you frankly before we went in the house."

She stiffened, having an idea of what was to come. For a brief time during the ride, she had thought maybe she could be happy here. Now she was wondering if their overtures of friendship were an act.

"My cousin told me of your ordeal and what life was like for you growing up," James continued.

Carlotta blushed, embarrassed that her tawdry past had followed her.

"You have nothing to be embarrassed about," Messali assured her.

"What happened was not your fault," Jean agreed. "I only brought it up because I want you to be assured that nothing of that nature will ever be expected of you here. You will be treated with the utmost respect a young lady of your age deserves."

"If you ever have any problems with anyone, please come to me," Messali said. "Though everyone who works here is like family, there are others you may have to watch out for."

Carlotta nodded.

"Your past is now just that, Mademoiselle Carlotta," Jean said with a smile. "We shall never speak of it again, and I hope you will someday learn to put it behind you as well. From now on, you are part of this family, and nothing like that will ever befall you again."

Messali nodded in agreement.

"Thank you," she whispered, overwhelmed by the support and open acceptance of virtual strangers.

"Good. Now let's go meet the lady of the house, shall we?"

She nodded and followed Jean inside.

Jean led her up the stairs to the master bedroom and opened the door, gesturing for her to enter. Carlotta stood to the side as Jean approached the bed. Madame St. James was in her late twenties, though her disease made her appear much older. Her back was propped up with pillows, and the children were lounging around her.

"Hello Yvette," he said softly, leaning to kiss her gently on the cheek. "How are you feeling?"

She smiled. "I'm fine."

Jean seemed to study her.

"Really, Jean. Where are your manners? Aren't you going to introduce me to our new governess?"

"That's Mademoiselle Carlotta," said James, proudly.

"Is that so?" Yvette said with a smile.

"Her name is Mademoiselle Boisvert," Pierre said with a bored tone.

"Mademoiselle Carlotta Boisvert?" Yvette asked.

Carlotta nodded. "It is so nice to meet you Madame. Thank you so much for this generous opportunity."

"Please, call me Yvette," she said with a weak wave of her hand. "And it is you who are giving me an opportunity."

"How so Madame?"

"It's Yvette," she reminded Carlotta. "Jean?"

Her husband smiled. "Of course. Come children; let's go see what Roja is making for dinner." He herded the children out of the room and closed the door behind them.

"Carlotta, please come and sit," Yvette patted the side of the bed. The energy seemed to drain from her once the children left the room. Carlotta perched on the side of the bed.

"Marietta has told us your story," she started.

Carlotta was surprised she didn't blush. She was beginning to become resigned to the fact that there would be no secrets from this group.

"I am so sorry for the pain you have experienced," Yvette said in earnest. That simple statement offered comfort to Carlotta. "You are much too young to have suffered through such crimes.

"I hope you will find happiness here, with us. In fact, I am counting on it." Yvette caught Carlotta's eyes. "I am dying Carlotta. I doubt I will live to see Christmas."

Carlotta gasped. Christmas was only three months away.

"When Marietta told me about you, I knew you were the governess we needed. You lost your mother early in life as well, didn't you?"

Carlotta nodded.

"I wanted someone here who would understand what my children were going through. They mean the world to me, and it hurts me more than anything to know that I will be leaving them behind. That I will never see my little boys become men or see Claudia on her wedding day." Yvette's voice choked as tears flowed down her face.

Carlotta wiped her own tears away, knowing what it was like to wish her mother was still around to talk to.

Yvette offered her a weak smile. "I see you understand. That is why I wanted you. You know what it was you needed or wish you had when your mother died. Do you think you could give that to my children? Would you be willing to love them?"

"I could never –"

"I am not asking you to replace me. I would hope my children would remember me always."

"They will. They will never forget you," Carlotta assured her. "There is not a day that goes by that I don't think of my Mama."

"I want you to love them as an older sister. Will you take care of them when I no longer can?"

"I would be honored."

"Thank you," Yvette said.

The room was quiet except for the sniffles of the two women trying to regain their composure. After a while, Carlotta felt herself open up to Yvette. "The one thing I wish more than anything would be the opportunity to know my mother. I don't know what she was like, what she thought, how she felt about things. My father never speaks of her." She turned to face Yvette. "If I could offer one thing, it would be share yourself with your children. Tell them all you can. Write it down. Give them something to remember you by."

"Help me then," Yvette said. "Help my children learn about me."

And for the first time, Carlotta began to think maybe she did have a destiny here with this family.

Carlotta easily fell into the rhythm of life on the farm. Once the boys were at school, she passed the better part of the morning playing with Claudia who then spent her afternoon napping and visiting with her mother while Carlotta assisted the other help with the household chores. When the boys returned from school, they visited with their mother for a half hour before Carlotta would set them at the table to do their homework. Afterward, they were allowed to go out and play until supper. Then the family, along with Messali who lived on a cottage on the vineyard, would spend an hour or two around the dining room table recounting their days. In the beginning, Yvette would join them, but as the weeks passed, her time spent at the table dwindled until she took dinner in her room.

After dinner, Carlotta would spend some more time with the children before allowing them to visit their mother prior to bed while Carlotta taught French to any of the Algerian workers wanting to learn or took a walk along the fields, enjoying the solitude among the grapes. Sometimes, Messali would join her.

It was during those walks that Carlotta learned that Messali once had a wife, but she had died two years after their marriage; he refused to say how. He had never remarried, choosing instead to devote himself to the St. James, his second family.

"A man can only handle so much heartbreak in his life," he said as the two traversed the grounds.

"The same can be true of a woman," Carlotta pointed out. While they all knew of her past, Marietta had not told anyone about Carlotta's condition. Carlotta knew that her disease would prevent her from marrying or having a family of her own. It was that knowledge that helped her open up so fast to the St. James. They made her feel a part of the family, and Carlotta knew that was the only type of love she could expect to find in her life.

"Touché," he said. "Is that why you never leave the homestead?"

"I've never had a reason to," she countered. "Not to mention, I wouldn't know where to go or how to get there. My Arabic vocabulary is that of a three year old and I can't read it. Besides, it's not like I have friends here. Not that I am complaining. I love my life," she said quickly.

"You don't ever have to justify yourself to me, Carlotta," he said. "And you don't have to watch what you say. You can trust me."

"But I really do love it here," she implored. "I have nothing negative to say."

"I didn't say you did," he said with a smile. "Besides, you are wrong."

"About what?"

"You do have friends here."

"Thank you, Messali. Though why you spend time with someone like me is puzzling."

"To me as well," he said with a shrug.

She playfully smacked his arm.

"Come with me tomorrow," he said suddenly.

"Where?"

"Some of the young men and women around the village go to cabaret in Algiers Friday nights. I think you would enjoy it, and you would get to meet people your own age. Well, close enough," he amended.

"Are you asking me out on a date, Monsieur Abbas?" Carlotta said with a teasing smile. She knew their relationship was that of an older brother/younger sister, but she loved to fluster him nonetheless.

"You are young enough to be my daughter! Of course not," he said, acting affronted.

"Hardly," she said grinning. "But it is good to know you aren't interested in corrupting the morals of young girls."

"While nubile sixteen-year-old flesh might be tempting to a man of lesser morals – "

"Seventeen," she corrected. "My birthday was last week."

He stopped and faced her. "Why didn't you tell anyone?"

She shrugged. "It's not important."

"You and I, Mademoiselle Carlotta, seem to have a different view as to what is important."

A knock on her bedroom door interrupted Carlotta's reading. Setting the book down, she gently called, "Come in."

Jean opened the door and leaned against it. "Messali said he was taking you to Club des Nassima tonight, yet, you do not look like a young lady ready for a night on the town."

"I don't know," she said. "It wasn't as if I truly agreed to go. I don't know anyone, I don't speak Arabic, and I haven't left the house before."

"That is exactly the reason you should go," Jean insisted. "You've been here more than two months with hardly any company besides three children and two old men."

"I would hardly call you old," she assured him.

"Even still, I am your employer, and I order you to go with Messali and have fun tonight. Make friends, dance, act your age for once. We will still be here when you get back."

"I don't know," she said slowly. Yvette had taken a turn for the worse during the last two weeks, which was part of the reason Carlotta let her birthday pass without mentioning it. She knew it wouldn't be long before they were saying their final goodbyes. That thought depressed her. It would be like losing her own mother again. Every day, Carlotta managed to find time to sit with Yvette as she wrote in her journal. Carlotta would tell the woman what it was she wished she knew about her mother, and Yvette would write the information for her own children. When Yvette's disease progressed to the point where writing was no longer possible, Carlotta wrote for her.

"She'll be alright for one night," Jean assured her. "In fact, she told me to give this to you." He pulled his hand from behind his back and shook out a beautiful sapphire dress.

"Oh, I couldn't."

"You can, and you will. Now get dressed," he ordered tossing the garment to her. "Go. Have fun."

He walked out, closing the door behind him.

Club des Nassima was similar enough to Pièce Verte to make Carlotta feel slightly uncomfortable. She tightened her grip on Messali's arm as they navigated through the crowd to find the others.

"Are you okay?" he asked.

"It's just a little more familiar than I would like."

"Oh Carlotta, I am sorry. I didn't think."

"No, it is fine," she assured him. "Really."

He studied her for a minute. "Okay, but if at any point you want to leave, we will."

"Agreed," she agreed.

They squeezed into seats around three tables that had been pulled together. Carlotta was quickly introduced to a group of very amicable workers and their wives or girlfriends. She was surprised how welcomed they made her feel and relieved that they all spoke French as well. Within an hour, she felt as if she were surrounded by friends. She had never really had friends other than the employees at Pièce Verte. She found the experience of laughing the night away, exchanging stories, and learning the life histories of these people to be time well spent.

They quieted down when the host took the stage to announce the evening's entertainment. Carlotta fought to hold her tongue through the acts she saw performed. While they weren't bad, they definitely weren't up to the standers set at Pièce Verte.

"What is it you keep mumbling?" Messali asked her.

"Nothing."

"Uhm hmm."

"It's just that I've seen better. In fact, I've performed better." No sooner had the words left her mouth than she wished she could take them back.

"Is that so?"

She swore the look in Messali's eye was pure amusement. That was never a good sign.

"Oh Iman," he said to the woman sitting next to him.

"I'm already on it." She leapt from her seat and disappeared into the crowd.

"What are you planning to do to me?" She whispered urgently to Messali.

"Nothing. Nothing at all."

Nothing turned out to be something. Apparently the show ended with volunteer performers taking the stage to belt out numbers. When Iman disappeared, it was to put Carlotta's name on the list.

When her name was called, she glared at her friend. "I can't believe you would do this!" she shouted angrily at Messali, who looked surprised at her reaction.

"But you have performed before."

She glared at him. "Exactly."

It took a moment for Messali to put the pieces together. "It will be nothing like that, Carlotta. Just sing." He leaned closer and whispered, "Reclaim your gift on your terms."

She sat glued to her seat as the host called her again to the stage, and the crowd began to cheer for her. It was the encouragement of her new friends that finally unstuck her from her chair. Though she felt like she might be ill, she walked to the stage. She took a deep breath and found that place again where her will took over. When the music started, she focused on the friendly faces around her and sang just for them. She let her thankfulness for her new life fill her voice as it carried through the room.

When the song ended, there was a moment of silence before the crowd erupted in applause. She bowed and quickly exited the stage. Her walk back to her seat was stalled by customers complimenting her on such a heart-felt performance. She blushed, not used to compliments, and tried to continue back to her table where she was met with hugs and praise. She was now officially one of the group.

Friday nights at Nassima became a habit, and more often than not, Carlotta found herself on stage. Each time was a little less frightening, as if one more string connecting her to Pièce Verte had been snapped.

She also began to get to know the other regulars, who were mostly other field workers or laborers. She was worried they might reject her for being French, but once they realized she was a hired hand like they were, she was accepted as one of them; only, Carlotta never thought of herself as a hired help. The St. James really did make her feel like part of their family, and she had begun to think of the children as her own wards to tend to.

All of which only made Yvette's death more painful. She died January thirteenth, getting her wish to spend one last Christmas with her children. Carlotta put on a brave front for the children, doing all in her power to console their grief. At night, she would lock her own door and cry into her pillow for her own pain of losing yet another mother in her life. Sometimes, when her heart was too broken to sleep, she would wonder the house and find Jean sitting in the darkness. Their eyes would meet and an understanding of loss would pass between them. More than once, they passed the night crying in each others arms, searching for a comfort and reassurance neither could offer as they mourned the death of a wife, mother and friend.

When Carlotta ran out of tears, she began to copy Yvette's journal. Wanting each child to have something in their mother's own words, she wrote for hours, dictating Yvette's thoughts and feelings into three new journals. It took weeks, but doing so gave her peace. She was fulfilling her promise to Yvette; her children would know their mother. When she was done, she placed the original journal on Jean's dresser and put the other three in her trunk until the children were of age to appreciate the gift their mother had left them.

It was a week later that Jean knocked on her bedroom door and asked her to join him in his study. Settling into a chair by the fire, he motioned for her to sit as well. "Carlotta," he began, his voice catching. "I can't thank you enough for my wife's journal. I had no idea - "

"Don't thank me," she interrupted. "It was all Yvette."

"No it wasn't," he said. "But I appreciate your modesty."

"I have copies for the children," she said. "They are in my trunk. I thought I would wait until they were older, but if you think—"

"No, wait," he said. "They are still too young, and the pain is still too raw."

She nodded.

There was silence as they were both lost in their memories of Yvette.

He took a deep breath and let it out, signaling a change in topic. "The other reason I wanted to speak to you is that I think you need to go back to having a life outside these walls again. You have mourned enough, Carlotta. Don't let your grief overtake you. It would make me very happy if you were to join the others at Nassima Friday."

"I don't know," she said hastily.

"Please, Carlotta," he said. "Show the children that it is okay for life to go on."

"And you?"

"I will be taking the children sailing this weekend. It was something Yvette and I always talked of doing before she got sick."

And so it was that Carlotta found herself back at Nassima. This time when she sang, she allowed her grief to seep through the haunting lyrics, leaving yet another stunned silence in her wake. As she tried to make her way back to her table, she was waylaid by a man she hadn't seen before.

"Mademoiselle Boisvert, that was quite a performance."

"Thank you," she said, trying to get passed the man to her seat, but he reached out and grabbed her arm. She immediately stiffened upon the contact, remembering what transpired the last time someone grabbed her in such a way. The man noticed her discomfort and immediately let go.

"I mean you no harm. I only want to talk."

"About what?"

"About what we do. About St. James."

"What do you want to know about Monsieur St. James?"

"Carlotta, what's the hold up?" Messali had come to her rescue, placing his arm around her waist and gently pulling her to him. "Hello Ferhat," he said coolly.

"Messali," the man nodded. "Are you playing baby sitter tonight or is she your reward for being such a loyal *pieds-noir*?"

She felt Messali tense around her at the derogatory term, but he just ignored the man and guided her back to their table, protecting her as they moved passed Ferhat. She looked over her should at the stranger who was still watching them.

Every Friday, that man, Ferhat, was there, and each time, he tried to approach Carlotta, but someone in their group would always be at her side, keeping her from him. After weeks of this game, Carlotta finally cornered Messali one night during their walk through the vines and demanded to know what was happening.

"Ferhat is a nasty piece of work, Carlotta. You are better off staying clear of him," he warned her.

"But what could he possibly want from me?"

"I don't know what he has heard or assumed about you. Judging from his comments and the mere fact you show up with the other hireds, he probably thinks you might be a potential ally. You are French, yet you are part of the help, not the ruling class."

"What are you talking about?" Carlotta asked.

Messali chuckled. "You seem so grown up that sometimes I forget just how young you are. Isolated here on the vineyard, you don't know of events that are shaping this country. Not everyone in Algeria is happy with the fact the French have confiscated our communally held land. Their interference in our country caused many of our people to become something akin to second-class citizens.

156

Sure, the French made us citizens, yet they took our land, our livelihood. And what did we get in return? We cannot vote. We have no property. Illiteracy and crime have risen. Our social fabric is stretched to its breaking point."

"What do you mean, Messali?" Carlotta said, suddenly frightened by his seriousness.

"I mean that the French have not all been like Jean St. James. Not all the people are happy with the current ruling government. People like Ferhat. The *Union Democratique du Manifeste Algerien* and *Mouvement National Algerien* have formed to call attention to the French control of Algeria and are fighting to gain independence. It is rumored that Ferhat is part of the *Front de Liberation Nationale*, a pro-independence alliance of Algerians who seem to be in favor of guerrilla tactics to meet their goal."

"What does that all mean?"

"It means that Ferhat is not a man to be messed with. If he wants something from you, it cannot be for a good cause. You would do best to avoid him."

"But what could he possibly want from me?"

Messali shrugged. "Information most likely. Unless he had somehow learned how close you were to the St. James. Then you could become a bargaining chip. But that is unlikely since most of the employees consider you a friend. But in times like these, one can never be too cautious."

Carlotta nodded. They spend the rest of their walk in silence as she tried to process all that she had just learned.

Spring gave way to summer and Messali's warning weighed heavily on Carlotta. She had begun reading the daily paper as well as any other periodical in which she could follow their discussion, a slow task as she had learned only basic Arabic. She eventually became well versed on the subject of the Algerian liberation movements from both sides. She noticed that Ferhat was never mentioned, yet each Friday he was at Nassima, trying to talk to her. She wondered why he was so persistent. What was it about her that made it so worth his while to pursue?

The answer came one Friday night in late May when Carlotta had excused herself to use the restroom. On her way down the hall, she found Ferhat on one side of her and another burly man on the other.

"Step outside with us, won't you?" Ferhat said in a perfectly gentlemanly manner.

Carlotta nervously glanced over her shoulder, trying to spot someone in her group to rescue her but had no success.

"They won't come looking for you for at least few more minutes," Ferhat said with a smirk. "You know how lines for the ladies room can be."

The men had escorted her outside the building.

"What do you want Ferhat? Why this game of cat and mouse for months?"

"There would be no game if you would have just spoken to me," he said. The other man just stood sentinel and silent.

"Fine, you have me. Now either talk to me or kill me."

"No one said anything about killing," he said with a wicked grin that made her think maybe murder was not a new idea to him.

"Isn't that what you do? Plan strikes, terrorism and such?" she asked defiantly.

"You are quite brave for such a young girl," he said stepping uncomfortably close to her.

She didn't back down. "I have survived worse than you Ferhat. You would not be the first to use my body, and death does not scare me. So again, I ask what do you want from me."

Ferhat looked surprised by her reaction. Clearly that was not what he expected. After a moment, he threw his head back and laughed. "*Ma petite* has quite the fire in her belly."

"Don't you ever call me that!" she hissed.

He looked taken aback. "That is twice tonight you have surprised me, Mademoiselle Boisvert. I will refrain from using that term you seem to find so abhorrent."

"You do that." She knew she was being stupid, challenging such a man, but the anger coursing through her caused by past wrongs was to great to stem.

"What I want from you, Mademoiselle Boisvert, is information."

"What kind of information?"

"What it is that St. James and the other French landowners are up to? Information about their employees, their security, their families."

"Why? So you can kill them?"

"I never said anything about violence," he said, amusement evident in his voice. "Your are the only one talking such."

"You didn't have to. I know enough about the *Front de Liberation Nationale* to know what your true goal is."

"The young always think they know so much," he said mockingly.

Carlotta turned coolly to walk away.

"Tell me Mademoiselle Boisvert," he called after her. "Did you enjoy it when Monsieur Riffaud raped you on the floor of your father's club?"

Her face paled as her step faltered. He was suddenly behind her, whispering in her ear. "He is here now. Playing the big shot in Algiers. He told me about you once. How you screamed beneath him. He seemed quite pleased about it."

She shook as the memories played in her mind, hating herself for it.

"Tell me, Mademoiselle Boisvert, would you mourn his death?"

Nearly two months had passed before she saw Ferhat again. During that time, she had continued to keep up with the news of the liberation movement.

She found herself torn between what was intrinsically right and situations like the one she herself was in, where the St. James had owned land for generations and treated the workers fairly, offering good pay as well as education. Jean St. James certainly was not bad for Algeria.

Riffaud was another matter. When she eventually worked up the courage to ask Jean about him, he confessed that he did know Riffaud bought property about an hour's drive away. Jean apologized for not telling her, but he hadn't wanted her to worry.

"You are safe here, Carlotta," he assured her.

Knowing that the man who abused her was here, she could somewhat understand Ferhat's concern; she could only imagine the tyranny to which Riffaud subjected his workers. More than one night was spent tossing and turning, caught up in the nightmare of his assault on her. Lately, just as many were spent planning out his murder in her dreams.

She wasn't surprised when she spotted the burly sentinel at Nassima one Friday in late July. He caught her eye, and she excused herself from the group and met him outside.

"Ferhat would like to speak to you. Will you meet with him Sunday?"

"I have obligations with the St. James on Sunday. Saturday is my day off. Tell him if he wishes to speak to me, he can meet me a half a mile down the turnoff to the village at three. I will only wait fifteen minutes for him," she said.

Ferhat was there promptly at three.

As Carlotta walked the five miles back to the house hours later, her mind began to formulate a plan.

"No. Absolutely not!" said Messali when she told them what she was thinking.

"I forbid it!" Jean yelled. "You will not risk yourself for the rest of us. Ferhat is not someone to trust. He will kill you, any of us, if he thought it would help his cause."

"Which is why I need to do this," she insisted. "He is out for you, both of you. I could never live with myself if something happened to you or the children. Please trust me."

"Carlotta, you are so young. You cannot know what you are doing." Messali pleaded.

"You both know I have not been a child for many years. If I have a chance at protecting the people who have been the only family I have had, I will do so. With or without your consent." With that, Carlotta turned and stormed out of the house.

The topic was never broached again.

Life on the vineyard returned to normal as fall set in, and the boys went back at school. Carlotta spent her days with Claudia and tending to her household duties. Fridays were still spent at Nassima. She had taken to going for bicycle rides on Saturdays, not returning until nearly dusk. When Jean asked her about it, she merely replied that she had ridden into the villages where she would do some shopping or visit the library where she spent hours reading. He had offered to teach her to drive the car, but she declined saying the bike helped her stay in shape.

In the early hours of All Hallows Eve, Carlotta awoke with a nervousness in her stomach. She only hoped she was doing the right thing. Picking up the phone, she called Messali.

"Is everything okay?"

"Can you please come over right away?" she asked. "And pack a trunk. You may have to accompany Jean on some emergency business."

She almost felt bad that Messali never questioned her.

By the time Messali arrived, Jean had awoken and made his way down to the kitchen for his morning coffee.

"Carlotta, what is wrong? You are going to wear out the floor with your pacing."

Messalli entered the kitchen, and she signaled for him to sit before she finally faced the two men.

"There is something you need to know." She urgently began telling them of her meetings over the past months with Ferhat, how she spent her Saturdays helping him plot against Riffaud, and what she knew would take place in less than twenty-four hours. When she finished, she pulled five ferry tickets from her pocket.

"You must leave. Today. I've taken my earnings and booked you, Messalli and the children on a four o'clock boat to France. Please tell me you will go. I need to know that you are safe."

She was met with silence.

Finally Jean spoke, anger pouring out his voice. "Why? Why did you get involved?"

"I did it to know what he planned. So I could protect you and the children." She paused. "I also did it to get revenge on that bastard Riffaud."

"Did you help plot his death?"

"Yes."

Jean looked sick. "You are not the young woman I thought you were," he said with disappointment as he stood up from the table.

Messali stopped him. "You know Ferhat was planning this before she got involved. It would have happened whether or not she was part of it."

She fought back tears at the look of disappointment in both the men's eyes, but she stood firm, knowing she did what she needed to in order to protect those she loved, even if they would hate her for it.

"Will you take the tickets?" she implored.

Jean stormed out of the room without response. She could no longer hold back the tears when he turned his back on her.

"I will see that they leave the country today," Messali assured her.

She nodded and turned to open a drawer. She set the three journals down before him. "These belong to the children. Will you see they get them?"

He nodded, pulling the books closer. "And what of you?"

She looked away, not answering.

"Ferhat will kill you when he learns we are gone," he said pulling her into a hug.

"I know," she said softly, extricating herself from his arms.

"Won't you come with us?"

She averted her eyes. "Tell the children I love them," she whispered before running out the door toward the field, the sound of Messali calling after her floating through the air. Only when her legs could carry her no more, did she collapse on the ground and weep freely.

Returning to the house when darkness fell, she was relieved to find the home empty, the tickets and journals gone. Wondering from bedroom to bedroom, she opened drawers and wardrobes to assure herself that they did, in fact, flee for safety. She said her silent goodbyes to each of them before closing the doors.

Settling herself on the porch step, she waited for dawn and for Ferhat.

The rumble of engines woke her. She walked calmly down the steps, her head held high, and met the cars in the driveway. Ferhat got out of the first truck and walked toward her, gun propped on his shoulder.

"What are you doing, Carlotta?" he asked.

"Is Riffaud dead?" she demanded.

"Why aren't you with the others?"

"Is Riffaud dead?" she asked again forcefully.

"Yes." Ferhat said. "Now answer me."

"I sent the St. James back to France," she said matter-of-factly.

Ferhat stared at her. "Search the house. Kill anyone inside and then burn it and the fields," he barked at the others.

"They won't find anyone," she said defiantly as the guerilla soldiers stormed passed her.

"Then you will die."

"I was always going to die," she told him plainly. "This way, I will die for something I believe in."

"And what is that?" he asked mockingly. "Love? Honor? Family? Some other high ideal?"

She shook her head.

"Then what?"

"You wouldn't understand," she said.

The men began to file back out of the house. "They're gone," said one.

"Carlotta –"

"If you are going to kill me, can we just get on with it?"

"You die for nothing," he hissed, pointing his gun at her as the men began to torch the house.

She shook her head. "I die for destiny."

"Destiny?" he said, in scornful disbelief.

"I told you, you wouldn't understand."

The shot echoed across the empty field.

Hours later, Messali walked up to Jean who was sitting outside his brother's winery and wordlessly handed him a newspaper. Jean's eyes were drawn to the bold print at the top of the page:

> *In the early morning of Nov. 1, 1954, the Front de Liberation Nationale launched attacks across Algeria targeting military and police instillations, communication facilities, French property, businesses and warehouses.*
>
> *An FLN proclamation was broadcast from Cairo calling on Muslims in Algeria to join the effort of "restoration of the Algerian State, sovereign, democratic and social, within the framework of the principles of Islam."*
>
> *The French minister of interior, socialist Francois Mitterand responded that "the only possible negotiation is war."*

Jean dropped the paper, ran inside to the telephone and frantically dialed home. He was met with nothing but a dead line. Sliding down the wall, he allowed the receiver to dangle as he buried his face in his hands.

"She's dead. Shot. The house was burned. Roja said the men were able to put out the fire before most of the crops were damaged," Messali said in a choked voice as he entered the room. "She gave me these before we left."

He handed Jean the journals. A letter fell out from the top one. With shaking hands, he opened it.

> *Dearest Monsieur St. James,*
>
> *By the time you find this, the world will know what Ferhat has been planning for months.*
>
> *I hope that one day you will forgive me for my part. But my reasons had more to do with you than revenge.*
>
> *I won't deny that I wanted to see Riffaud suffer as he made me suffer. He robbed me of my father, my home, and ultimately, he would have robbed me of my life. If you do not understand what I have written, ask Marietta.*

But that was not what made me agree to meet with Ferhat. It was my fear for you and your family.

When I first met Ferhat, he asked about you. He equated you with the tyrants, considered you the worst because you somehow convinced your workers that you were good and honest and that they were happy. You were a symbol of all he hated. I was aware of the FLN's actions, and I couldn't bear the thought of losing what I consider my family yet again. So I did the only thing I could; I became his whore.

I gave him my body, and he gave me information. He would brag about his plans, how the Algerians would rise up and reclaim their country in a bloodbath. When I found out about the plot for mass attacks, I did all I could to keep you and the workers safe. I fed Ferhat misinformation while I planned a way to get you, Messali, and the children to safety.

Please believe me when I say that I gladly give my own life for those of you and yours.

I know my desire for revenge has tarnished me in your eyes, but I hope this explanation will at least help you understand why I did what I did.

And please tell the children I am so sorry for going back on my promise to their mother. If there were another way, I would never have left them.

I doubt I shall live to see sunrise tomorrow. If that is true, know that I treasured every minute in Aïn Merane. Don't mourn for me, for I chose this path willingly. For once, I am the one in charge of my own destiny.

Yours truly,
Carlotta

716379

Made in the USA